PRAISE FOR THE WORKS OF
LYDIE SALVAYRE

"Salvayre's work applies a cheerful irony to very dark preoccupations. . . . Salvayre is a writer with a mission."
—*London Review of Books*

"One of France's most virtuosic young novelists."
—*Publishers Weekly*

"There are innocuous books that charm you, gently surprise you at moments you didn't expect, blissfully put you to sleep. . . . But there are others, like Lydie Salvayre's novels, that make you sit up and take notice, that directly confront you, that shake you up from the very first sentence."
—*Le Monde*

"Intense, claustrophobic. . . . This verbose three-hander twists itself into a tornado climax."
—*Guardian*

OTHER WORKS IN TRANSLATION
BY LYDIE SALVAYRE

The Award
The Company of Ghosts
The Lecture

Everyday

Life

LYDIE SALVAYRE

TRANSLATION BY JANE KUNTZ

DALKEY ARCHIVE PRESS
CHAMPAIGN · LONDON

Originally published in French as *La vie commune* by
Éditions Verticales (1999)

Copyright © 1999 by Éditions du Seuil / Éditions Verticales
Translation copyright © 2006 by Jane Kuntz

First edition, 2006
Second printing, 2007
All rights reserved

Library of Congress Cataloging-in-Publication Data:

Salvayre, Lydie.
  [Vie commune. English]
  Everyday Life / Lydie Salvayre ; translation by Jane Kuntz.
      p. cm.
  ISBN-13: 978-1-56478-349-3 (alk. paper)
  ISBN-10: 1-56478-349-9 (alk. paper)
  I. Kuntz, Jane. II. Title.
  PQ2679.A52435V5413 2006
  843'.914—dc22

                                          2006016853

*Ouvrage publié avec le concours du
Ministère français chargé de la Culture – Centre National du Livre.*
[This Work has been published, in part, thanks to the
French Ministry of Culture – National Book Center.]

Partially funded by a grant from the Illinois Arts Council, a state agency.

Dalkey Archive Press is a nonprofit organization whose mission is
to promote international cultural understanding and
provide a forum for dialogue for the literary arts.

www.dalkeyarchive.com

Printed on permanent/durable acid-free paper, bound in the United States

Everyday Life

1.

I read yesterday that violin strings are made from sheep intestines. I thought for a long time about that: how can music be made from such a brutal, evil act?

The new secretary's only been here two days and already I'm talking about evil—a word that's too excessive, that's just ridiculous here—and am already arming myself for battle.

My mind is definitely made up: I shall not relinquish the spot next to the window, the place where I do all my day-dreaming, which is no mere poetic image—I loathe poetry. When the workday is over, fantasy is my sole indulgence. All labor deserves its reward, Father often said. And I couldn't agree more.

If she makes a mistake, I'll order her, in a superior tone, to retype the whole page. I'll see that she types it a third time, if necessary. I will insist on that.

I'm inflexible about deadlines.

I'll only use harsh words.

Hurry up and finish those charts, I'll order. No, it can't wait, I'll insist while keeping my composure.

I'll correct her in a stern voice. The word *résumé* has accents over the *e*'s, I'll snap, emphasizing *é*.

Should she venture to ask a question, I'll refrain from responding right away. I'll wait until she asks again. Nicely. Meekly. Sweetly servile. How I'd love to attain that quality of disdainful authority over my inferiors that Father was forever trying to instill in me . . .

My coldness will prevent any friendly impulse on her part. I despise familiarity. In word or in deed. Informality should be reserved for addressing dogs, not one's fellow man.

I'll occasionally smile at her mistakes. She'll be at a complete loss, the idiot.

I'll keep her guessing. My tactic will be simple: each objection on her part will be met with unyielding silence. Keeping silent comes easily to me. Keeping silent is my job. Which I accomplish with zeal. Keep silent. And then strike. Ah, to have the audacity of real leaders! I've been inwardly training myself for that. After nightfall, when my thoughts emerge from their depths, I go back over what was said that day, her words and mine. I refine my tactics, reappraise my plans. I must be ruthless. It will be a hard fight, this I know. And in the end, our every utterance will be judged.

2.

Whatever her intentions (which I assume to be malicious), I won't let myself be caught off-guard. I'm methodical in all things (as soon as a thought crosses my mind, I'm in thorough control of its ramifications) and have a special gift when it comes to organization. I foresee. I classify. I pinpoint. I delete. I like things to be orderly. Monsieur Meyer often compliments me on this. And until now, my life has been—I dare say—as neat as my desk. Nothing ever used to go wrong.

But these days I'm filled with doubt and unsettled; I waver and procrastinate. When I walk past an old wall, I'm suddenly aware that it could come crashing down, crushing me. I won't risk walking under a ladder for fear of some new catastrophe. Time seems to shorten, then lengthen. Slippery as an eel. My soul is as sensitive as an exposed nerve. There are days when I long for my former peace of mind. And other days when the war I wage against her—and that's what it is: a war—excites and invigorates me, creating the sense that there's some magnificent destiny awaiting me.

The new secretary has only been sharing my space for a week, but already life doesn't move forward in a fine linear manner anymore, but sideways, tortuously, like a crab. Her presence is strangely disconcerting. I say *disconcerting* deliberately. I simply can't get her out of my mind. She's putting down roots within me, spreading, living, aching inside me, sending shoots into the tiniest cracks. (Isn't it odd that I find myself using the vocabulary of love to evoke her, even though she has a way of getting on my nerves, and I've come to detest every fiber of her being?) And she's the one I think of, time and time again, when with my cheek up against the windowpane, I look out at the street. Her enormous breasts. Her big moonface. Her beady little eyes, stuck in her face as if in lard, looking frantically around every corner as if something might jump out at her. I watch the cars go by, honking their horns. I count twelve of them. A bride flashes by, smothered in armfuls of white flowers. My heart sinks as I imagine her nuptial night. On the sidewalk across the way, two children squat playing a game of marbles. I hear one of them say *the old lady's watching us.* Yes, it's true, I am old.

I decide to go out shopping, to shake off the dangerous sullenness that's sapping my body and mind. In the foyer,

I glimpse Monsieur Longuet, a retired widower who lives on the floor below me. It's too late to turn back. I pretend to be in a rush, picking up my pace. With a sweep of the hand, Monsieur Longuet cuts off my escape. Who, he wonders, is the nitwit who could have dumped a deep fryer full of oil down the garbage chute? This is the question that has been tormenting Monsieur Longuet. The apartment owners are innocent, Monsieur Longuet would stake his life on it; people aren't so foolish as to undermine their own interests. Consequently, the obvious suspect must be some malicious tenant, and that's where the mystery begins. Monsieur Longuet lowers his voice. He's noticed that the two homosexuals on the fifth floor seem to be making themselves scarce of late. Not to draw any hasty conclusions, but still . . . Monsieur Longuet catches his breath. Some terrible disease or other leaves him hoarse and breathless, like someone in their death throes. With each gulp of air, it's as if an animal is crying out and dying. Monsieur Longuet must be one of those people who live with death. Just then, Madame Derue materializes out of nowhere. She withholds judgment on the garbage chute issue, since she doesn't like talking behind people's backs, but that doesn't keep her from thinking ill of others. So, we wanted to open up the building to outsiders? Fine. So, we wanted to be humanitarian and democratic? Wonderful. And now we're supposed to be surprised? Well, she, for one, is not surprised, not surprised one bit, and she'd go so far as to say she's been expecting something like this for quite some time. She tried to raise the subject at a meeting of the co-owners, but she might as well have been talking to the wall. So . . . if the deep fryer had at least been empty, moaned Monsieur Longuet in a long, two-note rattle. It's the oil that caused all the damage, exclaims Madame Derue. You should have seen the mess—it was all over the walls, the floor, everywhere. I'm telling you, it's pure perversion; there's no other word for it. When I think that they had to unscrew the hatch to the garbage chute, sighs Monsieur Longuet. What do you mean, unscrew? Madame Derue draws closer. She hasn't heard that detail. Monsieur Longuet assumes an air of self-importance. The hatch was too narrow to let the deep fryer down the chute, so they unscrewed and removed the hatch, though Monsieur Longuet still wonders how. It's downright Machiavellian, cries Madame Derue. And with that, she's off.

I can't bear this petty gossip. I attempt another escape, but Monsieur Longuet detains me. He lives for the few words he manages to extract from his neighbors in the building. It's his only pleasure. He clings to it. Monsieur

Longuet begs for conversation the way others beg for change. Just to get by. He inevitably reminds me of a dog, as the forlorn often do. Especially when they're poor. And old. With their dog smell, damp and stale. And their haggard look. An unbearable pleading look that makes you want to punch them in their soft bellies. His eyes: empty bowls, that's how I see them. And his heart, a gaping mouth that devours the scraps tossed its way. I avert my eyes. His face is fixed in an expression of insatiable hunger that compels me to look away. Something about him reminds one of death. I avoid him. I resort to the most shameful means to avoid him. Or flee from him outright. I always make sure, before opening my door, that he isn't lying in ambush in the foyer or lurking at the end of the corridor, ready to pounce.

I find this situation exasperating. I am, proud to say, fanatically polite. I believe I could subscribe to even the most dreadful behavior as long as it didn't result in bad manners. Yet I find no polite way to take leave of Monsieur Longuet. I bid him good-bye, but he doesn't react. Good-bye doesn't work with him. Good-bye robs him of his life. So he holds on. He waits, pleading with his eyes. I have to wish him a nice day, say I'll see you soon, see you tomorrow, see you later, and who knows what else. He just stands there, waiting. I talk about how time flies, how fatigue seems to affect the legs first, how impatient children can be, whatever silly truism first crosses my lips. He just stands there waiting. Finally, I turn my back on him quite rudely and escape. This little game has gone on long enough, I say to myself. But I've hardly taken two steps before he's harping on about this awful humidity that makes your feet swell or the looming American-Muslim war. Just rambles on.

Ordinarily, I avoid these colloquies, taking refuge behind a polite reserve that I know has earned me a reputation in the building as being arrogant, self-important, and morbidly rational. This merits an explanation, for such a misleading portrayal does me a disservice. I should point out, first of all, that by nature and habit of mind, I am inclined to be reticent, with little taste for verbal excess. I distrust phrasemakers, fast-talkers, peddlers of sentiment and drivel. They overwhelm me. I loathe base emotions that rise from the stomach and spill out of open mouths. They are malodorous. I detest wallowing in the gossip and backbiting that bind neighbors together. Such things sully the soul. I like people to be discreet and to the point. People who speak only when they have something to say. I can count those I've known on one hand. Father was one. Monsieur Meyer is another. Monsieur Eric Meyer!

Furthermore, I don't go out of my way to find friendly people. Friendliness disgusts me. Wearing the mask of a smile, friendly people insinuate themselves into your life. They pry and wreak havoc. Yes, friendly people take your slightest smile as an invitation to start prying. Friendly people bombard you with prurient questions about your spouse, your child, your illnesses, and then onto your private affairs. In the name of friendliness, they demand you tell them your best-kept secrets. They rush to your aid out of friendliness, because friendly people are helpful types. They ingratiate themselves out of friendliness and kiss your ass, while inspecting you with the thoroughness of a tax auditor. They believe that you're just like them. But when they stumble across something dark in you that doesn't match up with their idea of who you are, they run in terror. That's what friendly people are like. And the worst among them are friendly doctors, do-gooders, men like my son-in-law the doctor who attract the poor and the sick with their intimate doctorish questions, since the poor and the sick are so lonely and miserable that even the doctor's routine checklist of questions provides relief and consolation.

I must add to the aforementioned that I take great care to avoid any comparison between myself and Monsieur Longuet, whose situation could in some people's view seem to be the mirror-like image of my own—a cruel, unflattering reflection. I haven't the slightest intention of being compared to a retired widower, who's sick, to top it all off, and who arouses a condescending pity in everyone.

Don't leave like that, begs Monsieur Longuet.

His recent election as the co-owners' representative to the building managers has instilled a new feeling of authority in him that's gone to his head. I have to talk to you about our number one problem, he wheezes between two hacking coughs, the fee increase due to roof repairs. Monsieur Longuet adds a sentence whose choking sounds take the form of a strange syncopated whistling, after which he pauses to take a deep breath, exhorting me with a wave of the hand to wait, because he fears I might get away while he fills his lungs.

As if he's planned our chance meeting, Monsieur Longuet takes all the invoices for the repairs out of his pocket. He then makes a series of complicated calculations at dizzying speed. Twenty-thousand three-hundred and six francs, and eighty centimes.

Life is hard, he says.

You're telling me!

But you're lucky enough to still be working, to still be good for something, it's important in life to be good for something.

I smile apologetically. If you only knew how much I envy you.

Don't say that, for God's sake. Monsieur Longuet is skeptical. Everyone in the building is constantly reminding him how lucky he is to have so much time for himself. Can't wait for retirement, when we'll all be taking it easy like you. But I'm not an idiot, says Monsieur Longuet. I don't believe it for a minute. No one can imagine what an ordeal retirement is. No one, repeats Monsieur Longuet, in a kind of sad meowish voice. It's not exactly a laugh a minute around here, believe me.

I would give anything to be in your place. Everything, I confide with such sincerity that a hopeful Monsieur Longuet begins to believe it.

And I, who so despise those who display their private lives in public, I who've never exposed to anyone the sickness in my soul outside the confessional, I who feel nothing but disdain for the person of Monsieur Longuet, a widower with no means of support and who's sick, and who arouses in everyone a condescending pity! I find myself telling him in excruciating detail all the little tortures inflicted on me by the new secretary over the past ten days—her sneers, her snares, her wiles—her wheedling, adds Monsieur Longuet. Precisely, I reply. Nothing can stop the filthy, fetid flow of my lament. I hardly recognize myself.

Unlike my daughter, who loses patience whenever I start in with my sob stories, Monsieur Longuet doesn't seem to get tired of this account of my wretched little vendetta. He's developing a taste for it. Licking his lips. Fodder for a few days. He's coming back for another helping. Another ten minutes snatched from death. He urges me on. He seems to enjoy the most pathetic little details.

I even dream about her. Now what do you make of that?

I understand perfectly.

She has fat thighs, which she keeps slightly spread to avoid the itching caused by her sweating skin. Monsieur Longuet winces in disgust. Her skin is nauseatingly white; she's blonde. Monsieur Longuet is overcome. Have you noticed that a pale complexion is generally the harbinger of unhappiness, relentless grudges, gastric disorders, and cheap poetry? Monsieur Longuet nods furiously in assent. And if you only knew how she treated me!

No! That's too much, Monsieur Longuet bursts out in a great bronchial uproar. (Christ, I'll never get used to that racket.) You have to defend yourself, for goodness' sake, he chokes. (All of a sudden I'm afraid that he's going to drop dead, right there in front of me on the staircase.) You can't let an insect like her upset you. She has to be put in her place, for goodness' sake. If it were me, I'd show her who's boss, he mutters, nearly breathless.

After this series of implosions, Monsieur Longuet invites me into the flat for a drink. A little plum liqueur, something to pep you up. No thank you, I don't drink, I've never even had a drop of alcohol, and at my age, I'm not about to start. Well then, a little orange soda, a little mint syrup? I hesitate. But he looks so eager, so needy, that I'm compelled to refuse. No thank you. My daughter is waiting for me. Ah, children, children.

3.

I am hardly back home for a moment when I start wishing I had spoken about the new secretary more accurately. I have yet to figure out how to isolate the essence of her being. I put too much passion in my portrayal of her, too much hate.

And yet my adversary must be assessed, that's a rule in the art of warfare. Watch her, delve into her, scrutinize her from every angle, calculate her capacity to search and destroy. So that when the time comes, I'll be ready to attack.

I start again. I try to define her.

What she hates:

She hates elegant women who think they're really something special; who do they think they are? It's easy to look fabulous when you've got the body for it!

She hates happy people because they're nothing but liars, bosses because they drain you dry, the rich because they're arrogant, the poor because they're not.

She hates dogs because they make a mess, artists for the same reason, and worst of all poets: why don't they just get a job and make themselves useful?

She hates Charles Trenet, which is simply unforgivable.

List to be completed later.

What she likes:

She likes her husband, her son, her brother, and her mother. She'd give her right arm for them, and maybe the left one too. Her son's name is Steve (after Steve McQueen). For yesterday's lunch, she made him tuna in tomato sauce. Fish is delish, she joked, and they giggled together. Her son wants to go into electronics; she's all for his pursuing this cutting-edge profession. She helps him with his homework every evening. He goes to the School of Our Lady (it's more highly ranked than the public schools that are chock-full of riffraff). She tells him not to let anyone borrow his bike: don't let me hear someday that you let someone borrow your bike. If his report card is good, she gives him twenty francs, and what does he do instead of spending it on candy? He puts it in his piggy bank. Last Monday she went to see *Starmania* with him. Her son keeps her young. But why on earth, I ask myself, are mean, thankless, petty, uncouth people allowed to raise children? (And I employ that verb in its most vertical sense.)

Miscellaneous:

Her cruelty concealed beneath the fat of her face.

Her basic, incurable ineptitude when it comes to the life of the mind.

Her fondness for the superlative.

She pronounces *champagne* with an English accent (appalling).

It's impossible to look deep into her eyes. They're so shallow I immediately see the bottom.

This morning when I get to work, she greets me with: I found the light on in the hallway. She has that hard look of disapproval. I feel guilty.

Later she questions me: I wonder who it is that makes such a mess in the ladies room? Seriously. I mean, who on earth could it be?

I beg your pardon? There are statements that I simply refuse to hear. So she repeats them. I think I'm starting to lose my patience.

And I'm already sorry to be putting all this into words. These few thoughts debase me more than they discredit her. This is how it is each time I get the urge to describe her. Should I resolve to hold my peace once and for all?

Talking about her invariably ends in my loathing myself.

4.

I omitted one detail. She stinks.

The new secretary wears a vetiver scent, and I detest the smell of vetiver. There's nothing I detest more in the world than the smell of vetiver (after milk). It makes me listless, it gives me the vapors, migraine headaches. It makes me dizzy, nauseous. It makes me vomit.

Every morning when I crack open the door to my office, the obnoxious stench of her perfume smacks me in the face. I stagger. I can't help it, I've grown allergic to it. Like a police dog, I could sniff out its trail miles away, that's how allergic I've become. It's crossed my mind that she might soak herself in the stuff just to put me off, to make me go in the opposite direction.

But how in God's name can I get away from the new secretary and her loathsome smell when fate condemns us to share the same enclosure? How am I to withstand her repulsive, reeking obesity? How is one to battle the intangible, fight the very air one breathes? Shut myself in the ladies room at regular intervals? I've seriously considered it. But that would amount to swapping one annoyance for another. And what might people think? Or I could just hold my nose. An awkward gesture, incompatible with the decorum required of my station, and liable to jeopardize the smooth rhythm of my work. Demand once and for all that she swear off her smelly potion? The law wouldn't be on my side. Laws are hardly ever concerned with this type of harassment. They deal only in crime, and this is one crime that the law wouldn't recognize.

Monsieur Meyer enters the office. Thereupon, in a perfectly coordinated two-step motion, she sucks in her stomach and thrusts out her chest. She wants to appear at her best, I muse. The thought infuriates me. The EAU DE ROCHE—IT'S SECOND NATURE campaign report has to be finished as soon as possible; Monsieur Meyer is adamant. This is no time to dawdle, he jokes, before taking his leave. She flashes him the submissive smile of a martyred saint, which only heightens my fury.

I try to put her out of my mind. This cold war I'm waging against her is wearing me down, making me lightheaded. I close my eyes, and beneath the lids I see endless fields of black spiders—thousands, millions of hairy black spiders. My own visions frighten me, and I hurry to open my eyes to dispel this blackness, but then close them again, fascinated. Vast fields of black spiders have invaded everything. I think something evil has seeped into my heart. Then I conclude that the evil thing is the new secretary.

A noise snaps me out of these dark thoughts. SHE'S TALKING. I'd forgotten that she could talk. You can't forbid a person to talk, can you? Calm down, Fat Cat! she yells, turning toward the door where Monsieur Meyer just exited. I mean, who does this Meyer think he is anyway? Her voice sounds threatening. Just because he can throw his weight around doesn't mean he's allowed to walk all over us. She searches in my eyes for a glimmer of collusion, that odious connivance among subordinates. Just because we're lower down doesn't mean we should be treated like a piece of you-know-what. It's like he wants us to be his slaves! In the 1990s! I mean jeez! It's like he wants us to suck it for him. No way! she exclaims triumphantly. Not with me you don't!

I make no reply. I look out the window, out to a faraway sea. My sole satisfaction for the moment is to snicker inwardly at her outrageous inanity.

Back home, I run into Monsieur Longuet, tattered and smelly, his midsection thickened by ten rolls of flannel sash, his downy pajamas peeking out of his pant legs. Monsieur Longuet is on sentry duty. I suspect he waits all day, ear glued to the door, ready to pounce at the first sound of footsteps. He rushes toward me. So, you poor thing. She talks, I say, hand to forehead, as if in pain. My head is ready to burst. She needs to be put straight, hacks Monsieur Longuet, his face purplish. And with his fist, he fiercely mimes the turning of a screw.

All evening, I repeat his advice to myself.

5.

This morning she shows me snapshots of her son on the beach at Miramas, with his truck, with his electric train, licking an ice-cream cone, wearing his down jacket, at twelve months (the child is hideous); at two years and three months (hideous), with his godfather (it's her brother; the child adores him), with his godmother, with both of them; one of the school awards ceremony (he got the prize for most diligent), another of the school awards ceremony (?); of Christmas, of Christmas again, of Christmas, another Christmas; here he's blowing out his birthday candles (the picture is blurry; she made the cake herself), at three, being bored stiff by his parents, being bored stiff by his fat blonde mother; sneering (he was told to smile), at his First Communion (looks dazed), at four, at summer camp (she cried when he got onto the bus), at six, at seven—here the pictures come less frequently—with his cousin (his brother's son; he had to repeat a grade), with his grandma (my God, this child is ugly!), with his grandpa.

I cast only a brief glance at these photographs. As soon as she approaches, I draw away. I dread breaches of privacy. When seen too close up, faces invariably grimace. As does the soul. I cut short her outpouring of personal details. This smelly verbal incontinence of hers nauseates me. And so as not to subject myself to the dirty little secrets that inevitably follow the showing of a family album, I steer the conversation toward subjects of more general interest. I broach the topic of the recent census, which gave rise to some rather metaphysical discussions in my building.

We'd be better off if the police handled it, she says self-importantly. Because if it's left to *those* people (yes, with emphasis on *those*), they'll have us believing anything, any old lie they please.

Until now, I've never had to respond to statements of this kind. There's something repulsive about them that I can't quite put my finger on. Something hitherto alien that leaves me at a loss. I could imagine them in a Jean-Pierre Mocky film starring Jean Carmet. But in my office, no. I'm not going to be able to stand this. It's too much.

SHE CHEWS GUM.

I forgot to show you the pictures of my brother's wedding. She waves another envelope full of color prints. I wonder how many weddings and how many baptisms she carries around in her purse, and how many more I'll have to endure. That's my brother; he's thirty years older than his wife, and has she ever given him a rough time of it, poor guy. Just wait till he gets old; it scares me just thinking about it. (She's chewing away all the while.) And that there's my mother: she can't help crying; she was against this marriage from the start. And there's my sister-in-law pouting—as usual—on a wonderful day like that. Can you believe it? He's got to have a lot of patience to put up with her, poor guy, I'm telling you. It's not so much that she's ugly. It's just that she's so goddamn unpleasant. And there's nobody can figure out why some folks are unpleasant. (Chomp, chomp.) And calculating? I've never seen anything like it. She's a regular calculating machine. No joke. (She laughs.) And if you could see how she's got him wrapped around her little finger; she's got him right where she wants him, zing! And that's me, she says, with a haughty raising of enormous huge breasts so that they're level with my forehead. I feel a wave of nausea. You look good in purple, I lie. In the picture, she's wearing a purple taffeta blouse with puffy sleeves over which she's draped a white stole sprinkled with sequins and adorned with little pompoms at either end, along with a pleated yellow and black print skirt. She looks hideous. Simply hideous.

For the rest of the day, I fight the sense of anxiety those pictures have produced. Before bed I start reading an American novel my daughter lent me. If I can get into the flow of it, I'll be saved, carried away by other sensations, lost in someone else's memories, set free of myself. But I only skim the surface of my book, and all the funny parts arouse my pain and make me want to cry . . .

6.

Because I've had a dull ache in my chest for seventeen days, I go to the doctor. He asks me if the pain spreads toward the shoulder and along my left arm. No. It's just in my chest. As if it were digging a hole that opens and closes, opens and closes. While he's gliding his icy stethoscope over my chest, he asks what happened right before the onset of this pain. Imagine you're on a straight path, I tell him, which you can follow with your eyes shut, it's so familiar to you. Then, suddenly, you no longer recognize it, even though everything you see is identical to what was there before. Do you know what I mean?

The doctor is bewildered. He doesn't like being bewildered. To regain his composure, he subjects me to a round of thoracic percussion with the intensity of a drummer. I explain there's something that can't be detected by a stethoscope or other medical devices: a connection between the pain in my chest and the arrival of the new secretary. There I was, I say, the only one in my office for thirty-two years, and for the past seventeen days I've had to share it with this new secretary.

Uh-huh, um-hum, he says.

It isn't the arrival of a new person in my office that annoys me. It's this particular person.

Does that hurt?

Where?

Here.

There?

Yes.

No.

He begins to knead my lower abdomen. I feel nothing. Not the slightest little twinge.

I'm not impressionable, Doctor, nor am I very emotional. Long ago I got rid of the clutter of sentimentality and its accompanying over-sensitivity. Sensitivity, my Father used to insist, is the vice of the idle. I have an athletic soul, Doctor, toughened by duty. But as soon as I saw her face, a strange fear engulfed me. Not that there's anything unseemly or odd about her face. No. There's nothing special about it, other than its ordinary ugliness. It has a look of uneasiness about it, Doctor, an aggressive, quarrelsome discomfort, one that draws your attention rather than hiding itself, whereas I've always strived to disguise mine; she seems proud of her uneasiness, Doctor, *proud*; that's the word I was looking for.

Take a deep breath.

Would you like any more details, Doctor?

I take the doctor's silence as consent, and say I can see it all as if it were happening there in front of me. It's five in the afternoon. I'm sitting at my desk. I'm finishing the presentation chart for the TIMMY campaign. Monsieur Meyer opens the door and theatrically whispers: And here is our new secretary, Madame Barette, she's going to be assisting you on the job. And he did say *assisting.* So I look at her as she enters the office, slowly and massively, one buttock after the other moving forward, an unstoppable machine. I watch her settle in, taking up a vast amount of space in my tiny office. I feel myself shrinking. I think that I must do something. I don't move. All my senses are heightened. I catch myself watching her the way animals eye each other. I'm paying more attention to how she moves and yawns than to her manner of speaking. In order to impress Monsieur Meyer, she boasts about knowing how to use a Macintosh.

Having completed the clinical phase of his examination, the doctor sits at his desk and gets ready to begin the psychological part, the final phase of his examination. But the doctor knows nothing about psychology, and has no idea how to start the questioning.

So, Madame?

She has huge jaws, Doctor. I try to grab his attention. Pink lips, like calf's liver. And her body is hideous,

Doctor. And by that I mean the combination of her body with her mentality, her state of mind, her intentions, and not just the way she looks. She has huge breasts. Drooping, dreary, unappealing breasts that she points at people, not to drive them wild with desire, or tempt them, or to arouse their lust, but rather to crush them, to blind them, to smother and unnerve them. And I, who have always kept a cool head in all circumstances, I'm terrified, Doctor.

Now, now, says the doctor.

Is medicine of any use, Doctor, against the fear that certain people arouse?

Come now, Madame.

Monsieur Meyer closes the door and I'm left alone with her. Even though, as I've said, I experience a constant aversion toward her entire being, my sense of duty and propriety gets the upper hand, Doctor. Physically as well as morally. My back straight, one hand on the table, the other on my conscience; it's in that posture, Doctor, that Father encouraged me to go through life, and it is thus that I intend to continue.

As Monsieur Meyer requested that I do, in that caressing voice of his, I give her a brief overview of the Agency. Monsieur Meyer is the first in the world, and I mean the first, to have perfected the qualitative study methods for testing product mix, which have now become the industry standard. The CHOCOBOOM success story: that was his, I point out. CANIKAT, that was him too. He's the king of the ad campaign, I boast, to further impress her. SLYNKIES: SWIMWEAR IF YOU DARE! that was one of his. WATCH MOSQUITOES SKEDADDLE WITH SKEETER SKIDDOO, that was him, too. And YOUR CLOTHES HAVE A PAST: STONEGROUND JEANS, another of his . . .

Meyer, that's Jewish, isn't it? she interjects.

My heart freezes, Doctor. Monsieur Meyer, a Jew. But I attempt no answer, distressed though I am by this suggestion. I hate slovenliness, Doctor, or excessive sentiment. I have been raised properly. The griping and sniping of the great unwashed horrifies me. I leave that to my cleaning lady and her kind. If I'm annoyed by some comment, I give a mental shrug and let nothing show. If I'm pleased by another, I conceal my delight in the depths of my heart. A great show of emotion seems as vulgar to me as spitting. I strive to keep a grip on myself, Doctor. I do my best to be calm and courteous. Father taught me to be courteous toward the creatures who speak to me, be they below my station or above, and most particularly toward the uncouth. The uncouth are more in need of forgiveness than others, Father's sense of mercy led him to say. I do my best to maintain composure, as I was saying, and once my distress has subsided, I explain to her, as if she had said nothing, that Monsieur Meyer is of Alsatian origin. A seasoned entrepreneur, a consummate businessman. Always on the go, tireless. A man held in the highest esteem by no less than the President of the Republic himself. She smiles mockingly. A leader. The way leaders used to be, undaunted by trade union representatives, never trying to get chummy with them by talking about soccer. Affable, resolute, plenipotentiary, prominent. He gives his all. All the way, eh? she snickers stupidly. I don't so much as blink. He speaks to all his employees with extreme unction, I joke. Not even a smile from her. He calls me Suzanne, I add. Don't you think he's the spitting image of Sacha Distel? All the time I'm talking, I have the vague impression that I should be handling her differently. But I can't quite find the right register.

Well, you still can't tell me that Meyer isn't a Jewish name, she mutters.

At that precise moment, Doctor, I felt for the first time those strange clenching feelings around my heart and a dull ache with every beat.

Meyer's a Jewish name, as far as I know.

I'm well-behaved, Doctor. I mean, I know the meaning of restraint. And I restrain myself from acknowledging this lie. In order to keep the situation under control, I pursue my detailed commentary of the TIMMY account. The TIMMY brand, I continue—hosiery, socks, undergarments—decided to reposition itself so as to optimize its profit margins. But it became clear—after we polled department stores and questioned male/female focus groups aged twenty-five to fifty—it became clear that of all the markets for stockings, knee-highs, pantyhose, socks, and undergarments, the men's sock market first of all constitutes the best market per linear meter (I'm slowly regaining my composure); secondly, that it represents a steady market unaffected by seasonal variations, and thirdly, that the sock sector has just been totally revamped (I'm starting to get carried away) by the arrival on the market of fancy socks that are tending to supplant the solid colors which have had men's socks in such a rut for . . .

Could you please roll up your sleeve?

The doctor wraps the blood pressure cuff around my arm. It reads 150/100. A bit high. Cut down on butter and chocolate. The doctor advises that I come back for a check-up in a month.

7.

I loathe her, I loathe her, I loathe her.

8.

I loathe her.

You *love* her?

My daughter never listens to me. She doesn't understand me. I'm inclined to interpret this refusal to understand me as somehow a lack of love. You're getting all
worked up for nothing, she says, annoyed, as soon as I
begin to talk about the new secretary. She's a secretary,
not Godzilla, she naively complains. Make an effort, try
to be nicer; that's what my own daughter says when I
come to her with my problems.

My daughter and I are growing apart. I can tell by
a thousand little signs that only I can recognize. We're
growing apart: I haven't been able get that idea out of my
mind, and it breaks my heart. Sometimes I have the feeling that my very presence hurts her, gets on her nerves.
And the more I feel that I'm annoying her, the more I fear
annoying her, and the more emotional I get, the more
entangled I get. I grow overwrought. I blurt out what
I should keep to myself. I say whatever comes into my
head, without thinking. My fear of bothering her makes
me more careless. If you could see how shifty the new

secretary's eyes are when she looks at me. If I could get her to bend a little, feel sorry for me, utter one, just one tender word of compassion: Mom, dear Mother, my sweet dear Mommy. If you knew how mean you're being! My daughter's face goes blank, and I immediately regret what I've just said. How, I ask her, can anybody attain such perfect mediocrity? And my daughter, stone-faced, gazes off at some point in the distance. I mean, can you believe this? Yesterday she claimed it was my fault that the Xerox machine broke down. Me! You know how careful I've always been. Yes, I know, answers my daughter, tersely. She need only raise her eyes to mine, and I freeze like a deer in the headlights. Yes, just like a deer, I swear.

Stop it, my daughter erupted. She threw down her *Paris-Match*. Would you just stop it, please! She looked like a madwoman. You're not the only one in the world who has to put up with crap, okay? she yelled. I exist too, you know. Keep it down, please, I asked her softly. I don't give a damn about your neighbors, not a good goddamn; in fact I hope they hear. Who cares? Her eyes were bulging out of her head. I've kept my mouth shut for thirty years and I'm sick of it, she yelled. I dropped into an armchair, my heart banging in my chest. Trembling, I lit a cigarette. And spare me your martyr's face, for God's sake! She turned quickly, walked out and down the hall, slamming the door behind her. I ran after her down the main corridor wearing a housedress and sandals, at the risk of being seen by the neighbors. I heard the elevator reach the ground floor, then her steps grew faint and disappeared. I went back inside to lie down. I was completely drained.

I've thought a long time about this. Today I can see it clearly, I was completely in the wrong. But if I scratch the surface, if I analyze it, if I go to the heart of the matter, paying no heed to anything but the matter's heart, it becomes apparent that the only truly guilty party is the new secretary. She's the one who's turned me into this sickly, self-obsessed wreck, blind to the unhappiness of my own child.

For my daughter is unhappy, something I forget too often since the new secretary came into my life. My daughter married an admirable doctor, a benefactor of humanity who devotes himself body and soul to his life-saving mission. At the crack of dawn, he rushes off to his ward, does his rounds escorted by a host of nurses, like some sovereign, magnanimously distributing words of comfort to the crippled, encouraging weeping widows to busy themselves with matters of life insurance to distract them from their tears, and uttering noble speeches to families in mourning with such oratorical flair that he even moves himself—speeches that of course introduce the inevitability of death, the donations that families can make to the National Institute for Heart Research, payment acceptable by cash or check, and the ideals toward which one must strive with all one's will to sublimate the irremediable loss. At these words, the mourning families burst into tears and take out their handkerchiefs, and my son-in-law watches their twisted faces as they wipe away the snot, waiting for it all to pass, because, as he says, all things shall pass. And by the time my son-in-law the doctor gets home at nightfall, he's on edge. Really on edge. You're hopeless, he says to my daughter at her first little mistake. You left the faucet running again, he shouts, without raising his voice, since it's his eyes, dear Lord, that do the shouting. And if my daughter attempts to distract him from his hard day on the job by engaging him in a discussion on, say, the government's unemployment policy, you're wrong, he says, cutting her off before she's even finished her sentence; you have no idea what you're talking about (I think he has a mistress); you're too thick to understand anything (I think he hates her). And once he's spat out his two or three bits of nastiness for the day, he lies down on his back and falls asleep, mouth agape.

I think my daughter is afraid of him. My daughter is afraid of the Great Benefactor. So I console her and advise her and guide her. Don't do something foolish like divorce him and have to live alone; at your age a woman needs support. You don't want to end up like me, with no one to laugh with at Monsieur Longuet's ten layers of flannel sash, no one to offer me a gold watch with a tiny rectangular dial, numbers in Gothic, no one to call me Sue, O Susannah, Susie, my dear, my love, my little lamb, my life, my heart, no one to tell me that my green dress makes me look like an asparagus spear—why don't you wear a belt to show off your waist?—no one to go with me to the cemetery on All Saints Day, no one to defend me from the new secretary's brutality, no one to keep me awake with his snoring, no one to keep me at home with his fits of jealousy, no one to scold me, to brutalize me, make me suffer, Lord Jesus, no one to irritate me with his annoying little quirks, no one to go talk to the landlord about the rent hike, no one to give me the little bit of love you need to make life bearable, and if there's a war, what will become of me? No one to carry me, no one to hug me, no one to mold my body with his in bed, no one at night to gently split me in half like a fruit, O daughter of mine, excuse me, I shouldn't be saying such indecent things; it's not the kind of thing a proper mother should be saying to her child, but can't you see my heart is overflowing? You can't spend a lifetime dreaming madly about love and never have it come; don't look at me with those eyes, you make me sad, and ever since the new secretary . . . My daughter stops me there, staring steely eyed. Put up with him, honey; deep down, he's not so bad, and with time all cares fade, like everything else.

I was hoping this week off with my daughter at the family vacation house in the Landes where we go every August would mark a cease-fire in the cruelty of our daily exchanges, and would grant us the sweetness and rest I had been longing for these past months.

But dreams can deceive. Nothing turned out as it had in my dreams.

9.

From day one, my daughter orders me to rest in such a stern tone of voice that I dare not engage in the slightest activity. I can see that I'm in for a forced vacation, a week of programmed inertia that deprives me of the use of my limbs and of my heart, one that stifles me, makes me feel utterly useless, disposable. I sit slumped in an armchair for hours on end, mulling over the same words. She blamed me for the breakdown of the Xerox machine. All day long, I repeat the same sentence: she blamed me for the breakdown of the Xerox machine. And the more I turn it over in my mind, meticulously pick apart the accusation and review its minutest details to better discern its infinitesimal clock-like mechanism, the more I end up pleading guilty as charged. Perhaps I mishandled something, with my nervous condition making my fingers jittery. In the next instant, I vigorously retract the confession. This time no mincing of words: I didn't, I didn't, I didn't. And I begin to devise stinging rejoinders that I'll fling at her as soon as I get back.

You'll see what I'm going to give her, I murmur.

Oh no you don't! my daughter shrieked. You're not going to start up again with your ridiculous catfights.

Sorry.

At lunch, my daughter and son-in-law the doctor swap opinions about one of their friends who's seriously ill. At each of my daughter's comments, my son-in-law casts his eyes heavenward in weary exasperation. Psychological factors in cancer treatment? Are you joking? he sneers. Where did you pick up that one? In *Elle*? Or in *Marie-Claire*?

I feel sorry for my daughter. But I don't dare intervene. To mollify my son-in-law the doctor, I ask him a few medically oriented questions, though I have absolutely no interest in the subject. Upon which the doctor launches into an hour-and-a-half exposé on: first, an overview of myocardial infarction; second, the several possible complications; third, the possible treatments (only one of which is exceptional: his own); and fourth, the prognosis. As his lecture unfolds, he relaxes, blossoms, gets carried away. By dessert, he's dazzling himself, and by the time coffee is served, he thinks he's a genius. My daughter's face has the weary, dazed look of a poet's wife.

That evening, we have dinner at an upscale restaurant. My son-in-law finds the saddle of lamb overcooked.

Dog food. He shoves away his plate. He summons the waiter in a loud voice. Heads turn in our direction. You don't think you can pass this crap off on me, do you? The doctor is outraged. He is a doctor, and should be treated as such. What kind of a moron do you think I am? There's real cruelty in his face. My daughter looks at her plate and silently apologizes to the waiter. I came in here in a great mood, and then this, grumbles my son-in-law the doctor, who proceeds to retreat into a pouting silence until the meal is over. As we leave, my daughter goes out of her way to thank the waiter. Oh, so they treat you like shit, they make me look like an asshole, and now Madame has to thank them for it. That's great! My daughter looks terrified, and I'm desperate for her. My son-in-law the doctor derives pleasure from seeing her like this. He's a doctor. They bring you crap on a platter, and you thank them for it. She thanks them for it; I can't believe it! You're so gutless! He scrutinizes my daughter with the attention of a sadist torturing an insect. You could complain more politely, stammers my daughter. Politely! he screams. With these thieves, with these crooks? You're really hilarious.

The next day, my daughter insists that I come along with them to the beach. I obey. Obedience is the first lesson in a parent's education. Once on the beach, moved by some unexpected attack of modesty, I don't dare exhibit myself in a bathing suit in front of my daughter and my son-in-law the doctor. I keep my dress and shoes on. I sense my daughter is ashamed of me, but she would be even more so if I paraded around half naked. I settle down clumsily onto a towel. To tell the truth, I don't like the seaside. And vacationers even less. They're sunburned, they're sweaty, they're happy. Which is to say that I find them repulsive. Once stretched out on the sand, my son-in-law the doctor buries his nose in a John Le Carré novel: *A Perfect Spy*. It's extraordinarily hot. My daughter whips around to face me, her expression contorted with anger. You're never happy, are you?

Three hours without moving have drained me. We head back home. I walk slowly behind my daughter and my son-in-law the doctor. My daughter stops every thirty feet and stares back at me with a hateful look.

I take the initiative to make dinner. I peel potatoes. I wash them. I cut them up. In cubes, my daughter orders curtly. I dump the sliced potatoes into the trash and start over, this time cutting the potatoes into half-inch cubes. Like this? I show the cubes to my daughter to see if the dimensions meet with her approval. She glances coldly at the potatoes without answering. Honey, I start to say, but I don't know how to finish the sentence.

The following day, I approach her, placing my hand on her shoulder. She jumps, as if I'd tried to hurt her. Why lose your temper over little things that don't matter? I ask gently. Why? she mocks. You're asking me why? And then she launches into a scene that makes me blush just thinking about it. My own daughter, like some soap-opera-drama queen. In front of my son-in-law the doctor, this imbecile that I despise, she starts screaming: why aren't you ever nice to me? Why don't you ever put your arms around me? Why not, huh? Why not? And she bursts into sobs while her husband, my son-in-law the doctor, gazes at the ceiling, in mock resignation.

The trip back is spent in a dead silence that no one dares to break. I'm in the back seat. I watch my daughter. At each curve in the road, my daughter steps on an invisible brake pedal, then glances over at her husband with a cowering look. He keeps his eyes on the road, looking as though he wants to kill her. At about Angoulême, my daughter is seized by a fit of aggression and spins around in her seat. How long are you going to sulk? And a few minutes later: so has this turned into an obsession, or what? I hold back the tears. My daughter doesn't love me, I'm thinking. How can I survive this sorrow? It's going to give me heart failure. And yet here I am, still alive.

As soon as I'm home, I throw myself onto the bed. I bury my head in the sheets and cry. At five the next morning, I get up. I go to the window. The street is hushed. I experience the sweet sensation of getting an extra bit of life, life snatched from the night, a brief moment of youth. Heavy sleeper that I am, my dream life only begins at sunrise.

For the first time in my life, I'm late for work.

About her talent for underhanded whistle-blowing? She phones Monsieur Meyer to report me for being late. She's extremely worried. It's nine-thirty and I haven't shown up yet. She's warning Monsieur Meyer that something serious must have happened, that she fears some kind of accident.

From now on, in order to guard against her malice, I'll have to devise some fresh maneuvers, deploy new strategies, come up with new weapons. These thoughts continue to haunt me for some time.

I spend the night dreaming of warrior maidens, who torture me as they please.

10.

I would like to get stronger, to assert myself, to harm
her, Doctor. Draw taut my resolve like a bowstring and
launch an arrow at her that says no. NO. For the moment,
I'm incapable of putting up the slightest resistance to her,
of countering her vileness. Her vileness, Doctor. Does
the medical profession prescribe anything for this sort of
failure? Are there crutches to support character weak-
ness? Each day she gains ground, inch by inch. Each day
the breach opens wider, and each day I retreat further.
She seeks out every possible means of hampering me, of
overpowering me, of controlling me. Perhaps even of an-
nihilating me altogether. The doctor looks at me a little
surprised. And to think I used to reign supreme in my office, I who answered to no one but Monsieur Meyer and
my conscience (the two always perfectly attuned), I who
performed my job day in and day out with loving care,
I'd even say with relish, if I weren't sure to be laughed at
for it. I've become her whipping boy, her plaything, I say
miserably. I submit like a woman in love, I confess with
a pathetic little laugh.

There, there.

My seniority at the Agency and Monsieur Meyer's blind trust should have allowed me to wield the reins of power with a nimble hand, to imbue the new secretary with my own style, my brand, if you will, my work philosophy, you might say, to shape her like dough (I knead the air with my hands). But the situation has been reversed through a fateful sequence of events whose causes I have yet to fully grasp.

The more I think about it—and think about it I do, Doctor, constantly—the more it appears that her dull wit has interpreted my silence, in response to her vile remarks, as a sign of cowardice and spinelessness. And yet, Doctor, I persist in this silence that the unshakable principles of my conscience dictate I assume, and which I consider, despite my setbacks, to be the most intricate form of communication between humans. Silence, wrote Laurence Sterne . . . Are you familiar with Laurence Sterne, Doctor? He wasn't in your medical school curriculum? What a shame. But I don't suppose you can be in two places at once, now can you? So, as I was saying, Doctor, the misunderstanding between us deepens by the day. Between you and me? No, Doctor, I meant between the new secretary and myself. For instance, just yesterday she fires this one at me:

If a person lives alone, there must be a screw loose somewhere.

The remark is clearly intended for me. I don't say a word, Doctor. I have unbelievable self-control. And pride. I have my pride, Doctor. I bow before eminence, not before filth. Answering would amount to lowering myself to her level. Does one speak to a cow? To a sow? Nor do I react with my heart, like that poor Romy Schneider, who died of it. Even less so with my sexuality, as do some hot-blooded women I know. But with my nerves, Doctor, my nerves. I concentrate on my keyboard, inscrutable, like a monk with his quill; I let her remark fall flat. Plop. I keep silent, chivalrous, even though deep down I'm seething at such utter nonsense. For I'm convinced that those who require the company of others are often ruthless masters, cruel tyrants who demand mute subservience of their servant girls, of their bought-off spouses, of intellectual sycophants, so as to fill their solitude with noise and to release the venom festering in the depths of their hearts. I keep silent, as I was saying. But her stupid chatter goes on endlessly, Doctor. To stop her would require a silence of another substance than mine, a leaden silence, a sidereal silence, a frozen wall of silence that would stop arrows in flight.

People who sleep alone just aren't normal, she says,

salting the wound.

By now I admit I'm getting annoyed, Doctor. I wrack my brain for a quick retort that would shut her up. A little rejoinder that would be neither too cheerful nor too bitter, too playful or too cutting, too contemptuous or affected or humiliating. A conclusive and elegant reply. A trifle offhanded. An appropriate reply that would ring true. I hesitate. Hesitate. I hesitate so long that I come up with nothing. An idiotic expression comes over my face. I panic, praying to the heavens that I don't blush. I turn red. Because I'm the one who's ashamed for her, Doctor. I'm furious, disgusted with myself. My indecisiveness has once again given her the upper hand.

Anybody I ever knew who was living alone came to a bad end.

At these words, I should display the detachment of a tyrant, but it's not in my nature. Or I should answer back tit for tat with an equally disgusting familiarity, but my good breeding precludes it. (Never has a coarse word passed my lips, nor have I ever sworn.) I could knock her out cold with a stupendous slap, crush her with a phrase. Or think about something else altogether, my expression cold and impenetrable, victorious. But instead I cling to her words, as if compelled by some strange force, enthralled by the horror they convey.

And so, defenseless and disoriented, my thinking all jumbled, I set about nervously sharpening all my pencils, succeeding only in breaking off the lead. I realize immediately that I'm giving myself away, but it's too late to withdraw and start over. I'm getting flustered. I swallow my rage, which then swells and surges into that pain in my chest. And later, when it comes time to sit at that horrible, empty table, or in that stark, echoless living room whose wallpaper dates back to when I was married, or getting into that vast, deserted bed hollowed out by a single body, the words for which I had no response return, echoing endlessly in my head, and deep down I concede that I must be sick or insane to put up with this awful loneliness, this slow death. That's the worst thing, Doctor, all her evil thoughts have seeped into my brain and taken root, become my own. I'm telling you, Doctor, she's going to drive me crazy.

Now, now, she's going to do no such thing.

Another of her little ploys, Doctor, which she consistently uses to infect and infest my existence, consists of criticizing me for the least little trifle, which only plunges me into an obsessive dread of making more mistakes. I'll give you just one example, Doctor, the one about the coffee.

So as not to find ourselves in the highly awkward situation of each preparing our after-lunch coffee separately, since I never venture into those cafés that cater to all sorts of bohemians with their various vices, perversions, and contagious diseases, we decided to start a kitty and to take turns paying into it every month to buy coffee.

But since this procedure was established, Doctor, she is incessantly checking the accounts, making sure I'm not cheating, comparing the prices of different brands, her lips pursed in petty calculation. She accused me last Wednesday of not having paid for the month of October, though of course it had been a mere oversight on my part.

This pettiness leaves me distraught, Doctor. It causes my mind to lose focus, to make things blurry. My thoughts wander out of control, scattered like ashes. Could you perhaps prescribe some pills, Doctor, that would reassemble my disordered thoughts, make them operate unhindered prior to my opening my mouth to speak? At times, Doctor, my mind drifts, unruly, refusing to find its way back. At other times, quite the contrary, we become as one, it won't budge, and then each word she utters is truly excruciating. Her slightest remark strikes me like a slap in the face. My work is starting to show signs of strain, Doctor, I have to admit. Finicky as I am when it comes to spelling (I ranked eleventh in the nationwide championship organized by Bernard Pivot), I made a subject-verb agreement error the other day that is simply unforgivable. Worse still, I wrote that the brand GEO-MEC must capitalize on the "negative" dimensions of the Breton imagination: naturalness, the salty presence of the sea, the reassuring, conservative sensitivity . . . when I obviously should have written: the GEOMEC brand must capitalize on the "positive" dimensions . . .

I was sharply rebuked for it by Monsieur Meyer's personal secretary. Might the new secretary have turned her against me? I was sick with shame, Doctor, humiliated to the innermost depths of my conscience. She, on the other hand, was jubilant, Doctor, if you could have seen how she . . . No, no Doctor, go right ahead. Not at all, Doctor, it's perfectly all right. Take your time, I'm not in any hurry.

Dateline Strasbourg, from our correspondent at the European Parliament. Nelson Mandela had just spoken before the European Parliament. The deputies were rushing en masse to the restaurant of the Palais de l'Europe. Jean-Marie Le Pen and a few of his fellow party members were already seated at a table when two socialists, Robert Rieps and José Happart, walked in. Rieps let slip while passing next to Le Pen: I hope that Mandela's speech didn't spoil your appetite. The National Front leader looked him up and down and asked his neighbor: who let this animal in? then asked the usher to escort Rieps out. José Happart then stepped in and basically told Le Pen where to go. An angry exchange ensued. You're nothing but an animal, repeated Le Pen. And you're a swine, Happart retorted. The NF chief was seething and spat in José Happart's face. Wiping his face, Happart then threw the napkin in the far-right leader's face. Bernard Anthony got up and slapped the right honorable gentleman, who in turn countered with one swift kick to the groin of his aggressor, and then another when Anthony was on the ground. The two men were finally separated by the . . . I was reading the paper in the waiting room, Doctor. The news is simply appalling. You have an emergency, Doctor? Well then, I'll be brief: she is preventing me from having a life.

You ask that I get straight to the point, Doctor? That I address what's most important and leave out superfluous details? Important, Doctor? No, nothing important since the last consultation. My bowel movements are regular and my appetite is fine. My organs are all performing discretely, efficiently, like clockwork. There's just that pain, Doctor, in my chest.

11.

No.

If only I could scream out a *no* powerful enough that—if it were written down—it could replace all the words in a book.

12.

I have two passions that are really one and the same. I love numbers and I love order. I love numbers because I love order. It's my penchant for diagrams and for symmetry, and also my dread of change. To satisfy this inclination of mine, I count a thousand objects in my mind's eye: the floorboards, the jagged patterns on the wall, the golden stripes of my bedroom curtains. All the day's trouble dissolves in this mathematical exercise that requires no mental effort but rather an equal aptitude for tempo and abstraction. On a special little notepad, I jot down in blue ink perfectly formed figures representing my gas and electric expenses, all my rental fees, which I then add up, just for pleasure. I also keep track of how many times my daughter phones, fairly consistent from month to month. Not to forget food expenditures, which, according to my calculations, amount to a fifth of my income.

But this affinity that I entertain for things mathematical has altered since *her* arrival, the arrival of the new secretary. The attention to minutiae that once gave me such pleasure has turned into a nightmare. I've started counting up all the tiny vexations, the slow drip of the cunning humiliations that I've been enduring for two months now. I add up the hours I spend breathing the air that she pollutes, the number of times I raise my eyes only for them to collide with her ugly face. To that I add all my own cowardice, my foolish fears, the arsenal of verbal weapons that never make it out of my mouth, each aborted *no*.

And I observe with regret that instead of being toughened for battle, I am reduced by each new blow she delivers. I wonder about it. I want to understand. But every day, each of my questions flounders on a fresh injury. Could all the lessons Father dispensed with such adamant rigor now prove false? Is it not said that suffering is the refiner's fire that strengthens and hardens the heart?

My fundamental certainties are collapsing one by one. My entire childhood is being undermined.

One morning, absentmindedly, I borrow a ballpoint from her desk. Check the return date on that, she says sarcastically. Such colossal mistrust for so trivial a matter dumbfounds and infuriates me.

I arrive home, my blood running with rage. In the foyer, Madame Derue and Monsieur Longuet regale each other with the latest gossip. She only goes out to show herself off, whispers Madame Derue into Monsieur Longuet's eager ear. I can tell by her ruthless glee that she's maligning the pharmacist's wife, who wears red nail polish and pointy shoes. These are the people I live with: losers, louts, Spaniards, sluts, jealous husbands, atheists. The dregs of humanity.

At eight, my daughter phones. There's an unusual tone to her voice, feeble and elusive, with an edge that puts me on my guard, the insecure wavering of someone in search of an excuse and an exit. My daughter won't be coming by this Sunday, I conclude, and I go weak in the knees with emotion. It's looking like I won't be able to come by on Sunday, she says. I'm way behind in my work.

During the night, the spider visions return. I'm bathed in sweat.

Sunday is endless. I do the housework, little tasks, un-hurriedly. I have to make the time pass somehow, take little breaks, do whatever it takes to keep me going. I tidy up the medicine cabinet. With all the junk you've got in here you could open your own dispensary, my maid quipped the other day, in undisguised mockery.

Things do look brighter every once in a while, moments of hope, though I'm sure the peacefulness of times gone by is lost forever. There are days when the new secretary pretends to lay down her arms, days when our bickering seems to ebb.

She asks me out of the blue whether I watched *The Life of Chateaubriand* on Channel Two. She's making overtures, trying to cajole me, to charm me, to slither insidiously into my good graces. She's finally yielding to the superiority of my soul.

As a rule, I never allow myself to be distracted by such trivialities, a dangerous distraction from work. But recent events have seriously rattled my nerves, and I don't react with my same, hard-won self-possession and restraint.

Francis Huster's sideburns looked completely fake, I comment. And I burst into an uncontrollable nervous giggle. I haven't laughed for so long that a shooting sensation close to pain cuts my heart in two.

Those rosy lips and little slippers made him look like a faggot, she adds. I'm seized by another laughing fit, and the more I try to contain myself, the worse things get and the more exquisite the pain.

And his costumes, she blurts out, her huge breasts stirring in shivering waves.

Stop, I can't stand it!

I've collapsed on my desk, tears streaming down my face from laughing so hard. All the tension of the past few days has suddenly broken, delivering me from my gnawing anxiety. And I'm shamelessly draped all over my desk.

If Monsieur Meyer saw us like this, she gasps, between two spasms.

Monsieur Meyer isn't as bad as you think, I reply, slowly regaining an upright position. She flashes the cunning smile of one not easily duped. If you have a poor opinion of him, it's because you're seeing things that aren't there, I venture with caution.

Rich guys are all the same. She's back to being her empty-headed, earnest self.

With an uncharacteristic boldness, I reply: that's the opinion of a communist.

She gives a sharp little laugh. If it were up to me, there wouldn't be a single communist on the planet. Visine gets the Reds out, she sings to the jingle.

I wouldn't go quite that far, though it's true there's no love lost between them and me.

As if you actually knew any . . . She makes a tight little grin.

I do happen to know someone who holds communist opinions, a hideously common woman: an anti-Franco

Spaniard, unconscionably ill-mannered and uncouth. But she knows her place, and what's more, she's quite decent.

You can't judge from only one case, it's not scientific. True enough.

And as if to celebrate the unforgettable moment of spiritual togetherness: Why don't we decorate the office, make it a bit more personal, more homey. We could hang some posters on the wall; you know, one of those vistas of foaming waterfalls and green forests and leaping squirrels. Something wholesome!

Back home that same evening, I kick myself for behaving so casually. How could I have been so weak, so foolhardy, so quick to laugh at her inanities? That laughter was as compromising as conspiring in a crime.

I've reason to fear that she's trying to enlist me as a comrade, and this may prove even more hazardous than all of her animosity.

13.

I'd grown accustomed to her insipid commentary on articles from *Femme Actuelle*, which, to her contentment, would wrest an occasional mumble of acknowledgement from me. I assumed she read nothing else, and thus believed myself exempt from those absurd literary debates that are said to enliven the typical office lunch hour.

And yet, at yesterday's coffee break, feeling the need to astonish or impress me, or simply wishing to evade momentarily a chore that had her sighing with annoyance, the new secretary, with a look of bashful admiration, confided that she simply adored Benoît Dussert, who happens to be the most saccharine, inane, arrogant novelist of his generation, a complete idiot, a demagogue always ready to flatter his moronic readers. But, mistaking my stunned expression for some proprietary interest, she started praising Benoît Dussert's latest work, a huge hit, a novel about relationships that's really interesting, where this girl who's got everything going for her, and I mean everything, but who resists the repeated advances of a twenty-six-year-old guy who has done nothing but run around from one girl to the next. And so then, this young guy, when he sees that the girl isn't giving in, he falls madly in love; it's so beautiful. He does these unbelievably crazy things to get her to change her mind; he gives her expensive gifts, he pursues her abroad, he spends a night curled up on her doorstep, but she just keeps him hanging around, which only gets him hotter for her, until he can't stand it. By now he's lost ten pounds, he's going crazy, so he goes to her and asks her to marry him—I was in tears by this time—and of course she finally breaks down and falls into his arms. It's just divine.

I should have burst out laughing. I should have choked her with quotations from masterpieces. I should have spat my contempt right into her face. Put her in her place. But no, on the contrary, I asked her to kindly repeat the title of the novel, leading her to believe that she had convinced me to read it.

14.

I haven't told you the worst, Doctor. You know, it's painful to own up to one's shortcomings, even to a doctor, Doctor, whose ears, it would seem to me, are trained to hear such things. The worst, Doctor—I guess it's time to take the plunge—the worst is that not only do I cater to her every whim, but I've started going along with her, agreeing with feigned enthusiasm, rubbing her the right way, so to speak, begging her to teach me recipes (cooking is her favorite hobby) even though I never eat anything that doesn't come out of the freezer, forcing myself to laugh, though straining, at her pathetic prattle, at her awful puns, while my entire being is in revolt, and inside I'm screaming: you idiot, you so-and-so this, you so-and-so that, words I wouldn't repeat to you now. Can you help me understand what there is about me that brings out this sense of inadequacy? Can you tell what strange force could be throwing me off course like this, and into the orbit of this person who orders me to grovel—I who have never bowed before anyone, Doctor, except my betters? How do you explain this compelling attraction that has me bending before someone beneath me?

Would you like an example, Doctor? Here's one for you. Back from Easter break, I ask her casually and purely for appearance's sake if she had a nice time in the mountains. I expect nothing but a vague reply, no less a formality than my question. But here she goes launching into a colorful commentary of her vacation in an FVV. A what? My question makes her laugh. A what, a what, a putt, putt, putt? she mocks, with unspeakable coarseness. You haven't ever heard of Family Vacation Villages? I detect a note of scorn in her voice. They're as well known as Club Med and much cheaper, and the food's great—huge variety and all you can eat. And for the next hour, Doctor, she showers me with the disgusting details, without my daring to interrupt.

The high point of the Fun Fests, she effuses, is Open Mike Night. (I strain to look interested.) It's really great, you just die laughing. She goes pink at the mention of it. The point is that anyone who wants can come up and croon a tune, and the other vacationers in the audience think it's hilarious. (I smile faintly.) Of course no one wants to be the guinea pig, no one wants to go first, everyone's a little shy at the beginning, but then some old guy gets up to thunderous applause, wobbles to the podium and sings *La Comparsita* in a quavering voice, and pretty soon all the old men are up there singing the old songs from when they were in love, some of them act like vaudeville emcees and now ladies and gentlemen, here to entertain you at this wonderful gathering of friendship and joy, for you *señoras y caballeros* who've been anxiously waiting, I'm going to sing for you the unforgettable, the timeless romance of hearts forever young: *If it takes forever* (everyone join in the chorus), *I will wait for you* (all together now), *for a thousand summers* . . . The braver ones break out off-color songs, and the audience goes wild:

> You've heard of the gal from Seville,
> Who gives all the hombres a thrill.
> With a bump and a grind, she'll show her behind,
> And a bit more, to round out the bill.
> Yes, a bit more to round out the bill.

(At this point, I can only stare blankly. How can she not realize?) Some get all excited by the applause and pipe up with a second song, then won't let go of the mike, and the host has to grab it away and practically push them off the stage. I'm telling you, it's a riot.

Need I tell you, Doctor, how hideous I find the very idea of making a mockery of the elderly, of taking advantage of their disgusting friendliness to humiliate them?

And yet, Doctor, instead of drawing myself upright, instead of doggedly defending the ideals I hold most dear, I painfully repress what I feel deep down, nip my outrage in the bud, renounce it, tread upon it. Dead on arrival at my lips. What a coward I am! What am I afraid of, I wonder? But I keep going. I flatter her, court and applaud her, laugh at her improprieties whenever I must. I cave in to her despicable tastes. She thinks we're alike. I feign the keenest curiosity. I hear myself uttering: could you please give me the address of that, what do you call it? of that FVV, if you don't mind; thanks so much, so kind of you, thanks, really. And the more I hold my tongue, the more I want to tear hers out. It's a nightmare, Doctor, a nightmare.

Nightmares come from the stomach, you say, Doctor? Less meat and more fibrous vegetables?

All this nonsense, Doctor, would amount to no more than a few pathetic little incidents unworthy of interest if it weren't affecting my personal as well as professional life. No, Doctor, my husband died thirty-two years ago, which is the reason I started working. I began with Monsieur Meyer when he was nothing but a simple accountant, and I've watched him grow, expand, prosper, assume authority, magnitude, world-class status. No, Doctor, absolutely not, I have remained faithful to his memory. No, no one, Doctor. Monsieur Meyer? Doctor! You make me blush. Not Monsieur Meyer or anybody else. I've long ago forsaken the gymnastics of passion and the elegies to love. This might amuse you, but it's been ages since I've used any of my facial muscles to, shall we say, romantic ends. No, Doctor, your questions amuse me. When I say private life, I mean only my relationship with my daughter, my son-in-law the doctor, and my cleaning lady. These are the only people with whom I keep regular company, though our entente has considerably deteriorated, I'm afraid, since the arrival of the new secretary.

I know what you're going to ask: what does my cleaning lady have to do with all this? I'll give you a simple answer, Doctor. I'm using her to reeducate myself, to train myself to combat what has clearly become a crippling ailment: my inability to say no to the new secretary.

For instance, should my cleaning lady take it upon herself to move the hibiscus plant, I forthwith return it to its usual place to the right of the window, or better, I demand that the cleaning lady forthwith return it to its place to the right of the window, exactly where it was before. Put the hibiscus right back where it was, I command.

Here's my tactic, Doctor: nip each of her initiatives in the bud; it's with these little things that one establishes one's authority. For example, if my cleaning lady places a doily on the sideboard without first seeking my approval, I instantly, and I mean instantly, remove the doily and toss it into a drawer, in one regal swoop. Authority allows one no respite, Doctor: this is something I'm discovering.

If my cleaning lady says white, I say black, if she says dog, I say cat, if she says Marchais, I say Chirac, or I say nothing at all. In this kind of relationship, Doctor, authority must unceasingly manifest its ubiquity. Is it not written in Exodus, in the chapter on laws relating to servants: and his master shall bore his ear through with an awl; and he shall serve him forever? Any largesse will result in irreparable damage, this I know.

But there are times, Doctor, when we're distracted, busy with something else, stricken with remorse. When we weaken. When we lose our nerve. This morning, my cleaning lady took some little silk cushions that belonged on my bed and moved them to the living room. They look better here, she cried out, admiring the finished product. They match the color scheme better here, she added, searching my eyes for a glimmer of endorsement. I'm not made of marble, Doctor, I do have a heart. Let's allow her these meager pleasures that brighten her life, I thought. Let's not extinguish the pride she derives from such minor victories.

Obviously, my cleaning lady interpreted the magnanimity I displayed in the cushion affair as a capitulation. And when my daughter phoned to say she couldn't make it this Sunday (beset by melancholy, I had collapsed into an armchair), my cleaning lady proffered a remark that is unacceptable coming from a domestic. She said to me: your daughter isn't in diapers anymore; she can certainly spend a Sunday on her own without you.

There you have it, I thought. Here's what happens when nonentities are given trust they don't deserve: backbiting, the desire to get even, the rankest vulgarity. And as I didn't deign to reply: do a little something for yourself, she dared to say, with the insolence of underlings to whom the master has granted a bit of freedom, if only for a brief moment.

The line in the sand has been crossed, I thought. The hour has come. And for the rest of the day, I didn't say a word, as proof to her that the jousting had begun.

15.

While I was gazing out the window at the blue and green shapes of the bizarre landscape, the new secretary, dressed in a man's pin-striped suit, rose suddenly from her chair, swaggered over to me, grabbed me by the hair, and kissed me slowly, exquisitely on the lips. And even though Monsieur Meyer was surveying the scene disapprovingly, as would a father (I seem to recall that it was a framed portrait of him over the desk that was watching my every move, and not the living person), I couldn't muster up the wherewithal to fight off the new secretary, and I let myself slide irresistibly, like a swooning damsel, down into depths of pleasure.

I woke up laughing at the incongruity of this dream.

16.

This is indeed a first, one that will be talked about for some time to come, declared Monsieur Meyer in an emotionally charged speech, an unprecedented, trendsetting innovation of which I am the proud father (at the word *father*, a burst of applause), a move toward the future whose impact is absolutely immeasurable, he announced, throwing his head back as if to better embrace the future, an experiment that we are certain will be crowned with success (though to my mind, the crown would be for his head alone).

The film by Pierre Martin Jauffret whose title and synopsis we submitted to focus groups for the first time in the world, and I mean for the very first time, set off a veritable gang war at the Agency. On the one hand, there are the lily-skinned young women in black who swoon at the sight of the artist, and having been weaned on close readings of Eric Rohmer films, couldn't bear the thought that art with a capital *A* should be subjected to ruthless market forces; and on the other, the hard-nosed faction, sturdier, more numerous, and better organized, who, not wanting to appear less sensitive, assert with trembling voices that since art is life's highest value, it should be defended with a passion equal or superior to that mobilized to defend the cause of novelty socks.

As for me, I refrained from judgment, content to record and list the results of the study with the honesty and seriousness that are part and parcel of my being—I point this out without the least vanity. It is not my custom to intervene uninvited into my superiors' affairs. It's common knowledge that my greatest virtue consists in holding my tongue. And I look down upon these piddling squabbles in which idle peons seem to revel.

Les Passions d'Aglaé was the title put forward by the filmmaker. The focus group assigned to test its relevance and effectiveness was made up of seven women and three men between the ages of eighteen and forty. The ten members shared two characteristics: first, a very positive image of motion pictures, and second, an acute sensitivity to the values of the modern world and the media.

The initial reactions to the title proposed by the author were mixed. *Aglaé* was in two cases associated with pejorative terms: algae and something called aglu (whatever in the world that means!). Other associations had to do with a flower, a mollusk (unspecified), the female protagonist of a pornographic novel, a two-star hotel chain, and a modern young woman who is nevertheless deeply attached to traditional values.

All told, the focus group reacted negatively to the proposed title.

A few suggestions were put forward with a view to optimizing the psychological impact of the title, and consequently, the box-office receipts:

1. Choose a typically French name;

2. Go for simple over fancy;

3. Opt for a nickname, reminiscent of childhood, something tender, playful, intimate, such as Mado, Milou, Lola, etc.

4. In the final analysis, adopt a generic rather than specific term: *Les Passions d'une Femme*, and not *Les Passions d'Aglaé*.

The synopsis submitted by the filmmaker for the same group's appraisal recounted the adventures of a young woman who until now has led an exceedingly bourgeois existence, when she is confronted for the first time, on a humanitarian mission to Sudan, with poverty, danger, death and love. In a word, with life.

I must confess on this score that the various suggestions of the focus group that caught the attention of

Monsieur Meyer left me swimming in a sea of perplexity where I fear I'm still treading water.

Although I am not generally given to distrust, nor do I have such a lofty notion of myself as to suspect that people might wish to harm my reputation (I couldn't even remotely imagine being the focus of anyone's attention whatsoever, even as a target of hatred; I'm no Marilyn Monroe or Kim Basinger, convinced as I am of my rank in the great scheme of things as nothing more than a speck of dust, of nothingness), although, as I said, I am not given to feelings of distrust, I began to arrive at the conviction, or almost the certainty, improbable as it may seem, that I had unwittingly served as the model in the creation of the female lead in Pierre Martin Jauffret's film, whether for her physical attributes and proportions or her moral character: that is, I was her perfect opposite! A plethora of clues provide support for this conjecture which might, at first glance, appear unreasonable, but which grows more powerfully evident to me with each passing day. Take these examples:

The female lead, whose image had been described by the focus group and Monsieur Meyer himself, *is a lively, carefree young woman, exuding vitality from every pore, a striking beauty of youthful grace. The evening of her first encounter with the male lead, she's wearing a tight-fitting black stretch dress by Chantal Thomass that reveals her voluptuous shoulders and hugs every curve.* I wear support stockings, whatever the season. *She has a magnetic presence, she is brazen, headstrong, capricious, she belongs to the race of Mata Hari, Alexandra David-Neel, or Cleopatra.* I dress sedately. *She wears gray silk garters.* I wear cotton jersey undershirts. *She has an insatiable appetite for life, eager to fulfill her creative aspirations. She works out at a gym, goes to clubs, and dances until dawn.* I have never danced, Christ Almighty. *She seeks out the company of others.* The older I get, the more I loathe hugs and kisses. *She is not at all interested in the trivialities of daily life. Just being with her makes the male protagonist feel more real. He can no longer bear the duplicity of bourgeois life. Time spent with her seems to fly by at top speed; his meeting her has been a miracle in his life. Yes, happiness exists in this world. She is a member of an expedition organized by Doctors of the World in which she risks her life on a daily basis, but nothing seems to frighten her.* I'm even afraid of spiders. Every summer, I spend a week in Hossegor with my daughter and son-in-law the doctor. *Her bank account is vastly overdrawn, but money is a problem only for her greedy creditors.* I have a salary amounting to nine thousand francs per month, thanks to my seniority, and including my widow's pension I net a total of twelve thousand francs, so I'm not complaining. *She refuses outright any form of compromise or mediocrity, anything smacking of the shopkeeper or of life's seamier side.*

I could go on forever with this list of comparisons, but I believe I've made my point such that further evidence would prove superfluous. I can therefore assert, almost beyond the shadow of a doubt, that I have been used unbeknownst to myself as the inverted image, the mirror image, the ridiculous, detestable reverse of the adorable female lead in Pierre Martin Jauffret's film. Everything she is not, I am, exactly: the very model of the most twisted, inward-looking, reactionary prudishness. A scarecrow of a widow with a stone heart. A bleached shell.

Though tenuous at first, my suspicions have grown gradually with each new revelation of the study results, taking the shape of a kind of unshakable certainty that I am nevertheless reluctant to reveal for fear of not being taken seriously.

For the moment, I am unaware of the origin of this vile conspiracy that clearly aims at damaging my reputation and ridiculing me in front of my co-workers. Nor am I aware of the motive. Could I be arousing jealousy among my female colleagues, in spite of myself? Do they worry that my flawless comportment might serve to highlight the mediocrity of some and stigmatize the guilty conscience of others? Even though, at first sight, all evidence points to her (the new secretary), I feel compelled to remain scientifically objective and not to be swept away by a flood of emotion, which is what happens all too often in such circumstances.

I made the mistake of confiding my suspicions to my daughter, who, as I feared, was unable to weigh the situation with the requisite clear-headedness and calm. I've never heard anything so ridiculous, she snapped, testily. You're hallucinating. What you need is rest, and a good night's sleep. All this wild speculation is just a figment of your overactive imagination.

I'm even more convinced she's wrong since the new secretary's harassment, which I thought had run its course, started up again during the last few days, as if it were AUTHORIZED now—I'd go so far as to say ENCOURAGED—at the highest echelons. I am fully aware of the seriousness of these charges, and have thought long and hard before putting them in so many words, as I am doing now.

I have for instance noticed to my astonishment that our CEO, Monsieur Meyer, far from looking askance at the new secretary, with her coarse manners, her persistent unsightliness, her curlicues, frills, gaudy costume jewelry, and carnivore's appetite for domination, has on the contrary begun to show signs of holding her in the utmost esteem, and of taking more than a passing interest in her abnormal mammaries. I am surprised, even flabbergasted, that a man so worldly-wise, so preternaturally perceptive as Monsieur Meyer, could be fooled by her manipulative tricks. He has no way of knowing, of course, that she spends most of her time maligning him, calling him senile, a doddering, closed-minded fool, a filthy (one cough), a poor old (two coughs) and other such slanderous abuse that my modesty prevents me from repeating. How could he know she's incessantly complaining of his condescending ways, where instead she should be recognizing his exercise of natural authority and elegant restraint; that she's forever forecasting the doom of the Fat Cats, a generic term by which she means not men suffering from physical obesity, as I thought at first, but financial obesity, a condition just as damaging to the cardiovascular and neuropsychiatric systems as overeating? But when he's around she's all airs and graces, fussy-fussy, inane grins and flirty little pouts. And made up from eyelash to toenail.

I had rashly assumed that those beady little eyes set in

the lard of her face, that her mean little eyes would seem like mean little eyes to everyone.

Just the opposite has occurred.

It is her hateful baseness and the fear she inspires that have earned her everyone's respect and even friendship, something which I naively believed required greater virtue.

She's become particularly good friends with Monsieur Meyer's personal secretary, who I suspect is the main vector of this conspiracy, which I must do everything in my power to uncover, at the risk of provoking the direst consequences. I've observed for some time now that Monsieur Meyer need only leave his office for a few minutes for the two of them to be on the phone trading little secrets and recipes for dieters cut out of *Femme Actuelle*.

Within a week, as I was saying, the underhanded hostility that the new secretary had always displayed toward me was suddenly increasing by leaps and bounds, until it grew into a full-blown feud, which can only be described as: The War of the Cigarettes.

Before going any further, I should perhaps point out that, although I am in every other respect a paragon of temperance, I am afflicted by one flaw that I have not managed to eradicate despite the wise counsel of my doctor and the many dire warnings voiced for my benefit by my son-in-law the doctor. I smoke.

I smoke, and every blessed day I'm faced with the annoying fact that my puffing during office time has the knack of being considered an act of aggression by the new secretary, who neither smokes nor drinks, in the hope that her mediocre little life, her pathetic, miserable, by and large crippled—and yes, I'll say it at last; I've held back long enough, the floodgate is open, my cup runneth over—and shitty little life, oh yes: I'll say it again; I'm not above it—so that her shitty little life might last long enough for her to reach senility, dementia, and quadriplegia. I'm a smoker, but I take the greatest care (considerate as I am) to open the window every time I light up a Royale, after duly apologizing beforehand for the noise, the draft, the smell, the disturbance. Notwithstanding these myriad precautions, the new secretary, in order to punish me, does her asphyxiation song-and-dance and pretends to be choking, and this deathbed scene of hers only serves to annoy me further, driving my cigarette consumption ever upward.

And so, the extra work involved in the quality-control tests for the Pierre Martin Jauffret film, added to the commotion that their content produced in me, has caused my smoking to double, and I must confess my failure to respect the hard and fast rule I'd set for myself since the outset of our relationship: to air out the office at regular intervals.

Professional imperatives having taken precedence over all others, I have not been free to leap up from my desk to the window at every instant, as I probably should. Work being my sole concern—I'm driven by a selflessness that I'll refrain from commenting upon any further—I'm responsible for increasing the office's harmful toxins level by a considerable degree.

Retaliation has been swift.

This morning, I found pinned to the wall next to my desk a deliberately aggressive sign that I have no choice but to consider as a declaration of war. It read: NO SMOKING ALLOWED!

17.

I'm far from admitting defeat. I'm drawing up battle plans, and mounting the attack. I will crush her. She will surrender. I run into Monsieur Longuet patrolling the mailboxes. We climb the stairs together, one behind the other. With each step, Monsieur Longuet gives one of his death-throe moans. I'll never get used to that awful noise, dear God. Never. Once in front of his door, Monsieur Longuet asks me for the latest on the minx. Without waiting for my answer, he says: minxes of her kind need to be crushed, for God's sake. And with the toe of his shoe, he crushes the new secretary, imitating the sound of breaking bones.

Monsieur Longuet attempts to lure me into his apartment. Just five little minutes. Let yourself go. I'm not going to eat you, he says, looking at me with voracious eyes. I hadn't the heart this time to refuse.

His apartment is in the grip of unspeakable disarray. Every available space is taken up by yellowed newspapers, cardboard boxes, an old trombone, an antique shotgun, car tires, a rusted saber, a portrait of Napoleon, a girlie calendar, an old-fashioned sewing machine, bicycle wheels, a bathtub, and tools of all sorts organized according to some inscrutable principle. In a grand gesture, he invites me to be seated on the living room couch, which is collapsing beneath cases of empty bottles stacked one upon the other. I sit down gingerly, afraid of setting off a landslide. I nonetheless feel more serene in Monsieur Longuet's place than in mine, where, for the last three months, I've done nothing but dwell on my shame.

Monsieur Longuet hands me an orange soda, then pours himself a brimming glass of Banyuls. Cheers. Santé. Monsieur Longuet empties his in one gulp. It's just what I needed, let me tell you. He's pleased, and pours himself a second. He says with a fearsome smile, I'm one for having company. Something slippery about his look. I'm very uncomfortable.

So, what's the report from the front? he asks.

We're at a crisis. And if I told you the latest, you'd say I was lying. I pause for effect. She posted some antismoking propaganda right by my desk. Another pause. She wants war, she'll get war, I say viciously.

How awful, sympathizes Monsieur Longuet, as he suddenly grabs my hand and squeezes it, kneading it while his chest emits hideous death rattles. I wonder what etiquette would prescribe as regards the point at which I can withdraw my hand from this fleshy grip without offending him. I have never found myself in such an awkward position. My hand is clammy. An almost dramatic silence settles between us. I carefully withdraw my hand, and in the same motion, arrange my hair. I get up and leave.

Later, when I think about the scene, I decide Monsieur Longuet's attitude was quite peculiar.

I go to bed. Sleep is long in coming. As I stare into the darkness of my room, my thoughts turn inevitably to the office war. Suddenly a slogan pops into my mind: LET'S GET SMART ABOUT TOBACCO: HOARD CIGARETTES UNTIL SMOKING IS BANNED, THEN LET THE GAME BEGIN!

A second one then occurs to me, which I write down and post on the wall. LET'S OUTLAW THE SALE OF CIGARETTES: PEOPLE SHOULD DIE OF POVERTY, NOT CANCER. And although I'm in the darkest of moods, I can't help chuckling at my inventions.

I write a third slogan, then a fourth and a fifth. I write until dawn in a state of euphoria that has me all excited. And as day breaks, I've covered an entire living-room wall with little posters.

TOBACCO-STAINED INSURANCE CLAIMS WILL NOT BE REIMBURSED.

UKRAINIAN TOBACCO FIELDS WILL BE REPLACED BY NUCLEAR POWER STATIONS.

Every cigarette brings you closer to death. Smoke it at both ends.

Camels should be an endangered species.

No more Gauloise history in our school curriculum.

Before leaving for the office, I show Monsieur Longuet my late-night productions. I believe there is a glimmer of admiration in his eyes. But after scratching his forehead thoughtfully, he cautions me to be sly and have the patience of Buddha.

I follow his advice and, with no regrets, toss my slogans into the trash.

18.

I've been undecided for quite some time as to whether or not to attend the cocktail party celebrating the success of Pierre Martin Jauffret's film. I can't stand parties, and don't want to be ridiculed. The energy expended in trying to appear frivolous is finally too exhausting. A series of setbacks since the death of my husband has caused me to renounce the things of this world. And when all is said and done, I'm delighted with the result. There's something dishonest about these receptions, these tributes, these religious services where there is more perspiration than inspiration.

But I overcome my reluctance and decide to attend. The last thing I want is for my absence to attract even more attention to myself.

I opt for the plainest possible outfit: a white silk blouse and a gray skirt. The purpose of elegance, in my view, is not to do violence to the eye of the beholder. My daughter, when asked for her opinion, finds my outfit prosaic. She thinks I look frumpy. I snap back that I prefer a discreet elegance, which I suppose is a redundancy, since elegance is by nature and design the very essence of discretion.

I'm not your Almodovar, I laugh (a filmmaker that my daughter is wild about, and, if I'm to believe her descriptions, someone afflicted with particularly abominable taste. He is Spanish).

I am among the first arrivals. (I pride myself on being punctual, whatever the circumstance.) The crowd gradually gathers so that by 10:00 P.M. the room is packed. On several occasions, I attempt to edge closer to Monsieur Meyer just to say hello. But each time he gets snatched up by some frenzied female, some flashy tigress who's all breasts and buttocks and throws herself at him with sickening lust. The new secretary is decked out in a dress worthy of Elizabeth Taylor. Cotton candy pink with puffy sleeves and a plunging neckline down to her navel.

All eyes are on her décolleté. She swells with pride, triumphant. Has she any idea, poor thing, how out of place she looks in this gathering of smart trendsetters, promoters of goth aesthetics and media ethics? But I withhold any sympathy, for she's now leaning over to whisper to Monsieur Meyer's personal secretary, and I'm one-hundred percent certain, absolutely, that she's talking about me in relation to how I'm the perfect antithesis of the female lead in Pierre Martin Jauffret's film.

I make a second attempt to approach Monsieur Meyer, but the crowd is so thick by now that it's next to impossible to push my way through. Somehow, I manage to clear the way. Only a few steps separate me from Monsieur Meyer when suddenly Pierre Martin Jauffret springs up from behind and throws his arm around him and the two men effusively embrace. A kind of whirling movement is set off around them and I'm carried away by the madding crowd.

I resolve to wait until Monsieur Meyer himself comes over to offer his respects, as I know he undoubtedly will. I'm thrilled at the idea that he might introduce me to his guests, and I'm dying to slip in a word or two to André Dussollier, whom I so admire. On television, he is always so perfectly tasteful and exquisitely courteous, truly an endangered species among today's entertainers, who idiotically mistake swinish behavior for creative daring. I won't mention any names. My recent misfortunes have made me exceedingly cautious in that regard.

All around me, people are chanting the praises of Pierre Martin Jauffret's masterpiece, which, as they intone ad nauseam, has already met with resounding success. A man with perfect teeth (he seems to tear at the air with them) explains to a couple of the miniskirted girls that Pierre Martin Jauffret was able to capture so marvelously (his diction reminds me of Fabrice Lucchini) the *now* moment and the spirit of today's young people, who, unlike their elders, proclaim loud and clear their drive to succeed, and that includes (here he points his finger to the ceiling) in matters of love, and he does this thanks to unpretentious visuals and simple dialogue that any moviegoer can understand. The girls hang on his every word, trying their best to look clever.

No one so much as glances at me, and I'm not quite sure where to turn. I notice the Agency receptionist who is one of the rare people in this room I actually know. I head in her direction in the hope of making some small talk. But the receptionist looks straight through me as if I weren't there and continues her conversation with an elegant young man. The situation is becoming distressful. I move to the buffet and order an orange juice. I'm served a flute of champagne. Throwing caution to the wind, I down it in one gulp. At intervals, I cast a furtive glance in the direction of Monsieur Meyer, who has yet to extend me his regards. My head has started to spin. Monsieur Meyer appears deep in a lively discussion with Pierre Martin Jauffret. Then, at a precise moment, I get the distinct impression that both these men are looking straight at me: the perfect antithesis of the film's female lead. I abruptly become conscious of the fact that everyone at this party is avoiding me, that no one wants to risk being seen in my company. Within seconds, I can feel myself becoming the center of inattention, a negative center, just like my heart, which pumps a dark, infected blood through my veins, poisoning rather than nourishing.

I flee.

19.

For the moment, I simply observe. I watch her get bolder by the day, making her presence felt, making herself more comfortable. She has prevailed. Yet I still only observe. Through sheer concentration I have become sensitive to the slightest shift in the wind. I perceive the tiniest atmospheric changes, those that would normally escape notice, an infinitesimal deviation in one of her looks, an imperceptible tremor of the lips, a hand seeking something to lean on. I watch. Motionless. While I lay sleepless at night, all my senses are focused on my prey, and while my mind stalks tirelessly, ferreting out and scrutinizing everything horrible, I analyze her. My powers of observation have reached such an intensity that I can read her ulterior motives. I can second-guess her, as if I were she. I've heard that certain dire situations can sometimes give you, almost miraculously, the gift of second sight. A specialist on the subject of clairvoyance explained it on the *Bonjour Madame* show. Though I'm loath to admit it, I've even felt at times that I'm capable of reading everybody's mind—that an immense clarity has opened up within me, like a sun.

One morning, Monsieur Meyer bursts into my office with the look of a desperate man. Getting straight to the point (he who is habitually so roundabout, so suave, so indirect), he asks whether one of us might be available on an emergency basis to work all day this coming Saturday. You would be doing me a huge favor, he pleads, in his deep baritone voice. I can't go into details, but we're talking about something serious here: I'm bidding for a deal against Séguéla. His face is beaming with pride.

The moment has come for me to strike. To show her for what she is. The chance to definitively clear my name in Monsieur Meyer's esteem, and at the same time expose in a spectacular fashion her countless deceptions.

I am not one to show off my virtues. In fact, I loathe exhibitionism of every kind. Discretion is, in my eyes, the cardinal virtue. I'll go so far as to say that one ought to be discreet in one's discretion, a dictum to which, alas, I have not always adhered in my own life, for in my pursuing and achieving virtue, my fervor often gets the better of me, further heightened by my solitude and highly selective reading habits. I do feel, nevertheless, that in certain rare circumstances, it can prove useful to overtly manifest those qualities at which I excel and which everyone around me makes a point of eschewing, when they are not openly adverse to them.

Before the new secretary even has the time to react, I say yes sir, it would be no bother at all, sir; on the contrary, I have no plans for this weekend, it will keep me busy. I want to prove to Monsieur Meyer once and for all that I surpass her in loyalty, propriety, and steadfastness. In a word, that I have character.

The new secretary is upset.

She is extremely upset.

Monsieur Meyer is hardly out of the room before she's furiously crumpling up sheets of paper and hurling them into the garbage.

Then she utters the line that has not left my thoughts for months now: That's wonderful, just wonderful (little cough).

It takes me a moment to realize I've just been insulted. I experience an uncanny feeling of freedom. I now know that the end is near. And, short of a miracle, I sit back and wait for the coup de grace. Or grace itself.

For the remainder of the day, she fusses about noisily, maintaining her foul mood. She replies tersely to phone calls, slams cabinet doors, and manhandles files as if they were struggling against her. While putting her desk in order at the end of the day, she makes a pronouncement that I'm not quite sure I understand: If there's one thing I can't stand, it's a suck-up.

The following week is excruciating. She doesn't utter a word. No hello, no good-bye. Nothing. Total silence. At times, the silence is deafening, like the moment in horror movies right before a loud burst of music. Her fat cheeks tremble with suppressed anger. She paces the office. Each of her movements sets off a storm. She is everywhere at once; I'm surrounded. She's trying to drive me mad. I hate suck-ups, she mumbles on several occasions, as if talking to herself. I'm on edge, ready for anything. The slightest sound startles me. There's a bitter taste in my mouth, and that ever-present pain in my chest. But these troubles seem minor compared to my other torments.

Have you ever experienced the curse of being obsessed? I asked Monsieur Longuet as he surveyed from his window the progress of the paving on the street below. The same idea, day in, day out? The same idea, constantly, like a throbbing headache, against which willpower proves vain, helpless? An idea that never loses its force: do you know what such an idea feels like, an all-consuming idea? Whose capacity for inflicting pain is endless? Whose power remains intact, as happens in love affairs?

I watch her every move very closely. Nothing, I'm convinced, escapes my notice. And I exercise this same intense surveillance on myself, because I know that the enemy only needs one false move on the part of her adversary in order to surprise and defeat her. But self-control is my strength. I almost want to say that it's second nature. Extensive experience in self-restraint has made my face rigid as a corset. A mere act of will, and no emotion shows.

I eavesdrop intently on her phone calls, an exhausting exercise, because I have to reconstruct whole conversations out of the odd word and phrase. One day, I seem to overhear her say: we have to get rid of her. And I hear other such threatening comments. Sometimes I think I must be imagining them. The next day, I'm convinced that I'm not. And everything becomes mixed up in my head.

I'm afraid.

I often repeat to myself that the new secretary is living an ordinary life, the most unexceptional, the most common of lives, that nothing distinguishes her from the rest of creation, and that, finally, she is much less different from me than I would like to think. Still, I can't help but discern deep within her corpulence some dark force at work that might one day burst forth.

I am also experiencing an absurd feeling, one which no doubt contributes to my fear, that the world around me has become denser, heavier, more burdensome, as if the frenzied attention I pay to the new secretary's every move has added more weight to reality.

At night, I dread going to sleep, where enormous, hairy black spiders await. My eyes are like two raw wounds. Opening them is torture; closing them is worse. I've stopped reading, I no longer laugh. And it's been months since I've paid my bills.

I make a last attempt with my daughter. I want to present her with the facts in all their stark TRUTH. If my daughter is never made aware of these crimes, who will know the extent of my suffering and see that justice is done? I purposely assume a neutral tone in order not to alarm her. I provide a clear and dispassionate summary of the situation. I tell her simply that the new secretary is blatantly persecuting me, and I insist on *blatantly*, and that she is trying to get rid of me. Monsieur Meyer undoubtedly has a hand in it, though I don't have any proof. The tension has become unbearable. A spark could set the whole place on fire. I have to do something. Punish the guilty. The surprise attack could come any minute now.

My daughter is distraught. She says I'm overworked, on the verge of a mental breakdown, that I should see a doctor immediately. I counter that I've seen my doctor several times now, but that he didn't seem to understand my predicament. The idiot seems interested only in the circulation of my body fluids. It takes a profound knowledge of human life in all its crests and troughs to fully grasp what I'm going through, I tell her. Few people are capable of such insight, much less doctors, who are so uncouth, so stupid, so pretentious. I'm not talking about your husband, of course.

In an uncharacteristic gesture, my daughter announces that my son-in-law the doctor would like to have a word with me, and hands him the phone. My son-in-law the doctor thrusts his diagnosis at me: I'm suffering from mental strain, my nerves are shot, treatment is in order. I suppress the desire to hang up on him. Could he be conspiring with the enemy? Nothing would surprise me at this point. I tersely reply that I'm perfectly calm, calmer than he is, in fact, and that I feel fine, that I simply have a few problems at the office, same as everyone. The ordinary little problems that come from living together.

Mom, my daughter cries into the phone. The sound of her voice is frightening.

The following day, Monsieur Meyer doesn't address the both of us together, as he usually does when he wants us to give him an update on our work. He turns conspicuously to the new secretary. Exactly as if I were dead and gone. I realize at once that I have fallen into disfavor with Monsieur Meyer.

20.

I won't go into the outrageous sexual slander of which I was victim, nor the female cabals endlessly plotted behind my back. For a lofty spirit such as mine, scandal of this sort is of no importance in the end, and I delete it from my memory, with no feelings of resentment. But there is one hurt that I cannot forget, and that is the unspeakable attitude of Monsieur Meyer when I had my accident.

I'm still lying on the floor surrounded by my gawking co-workers who are struggling to suppress their laughter, when Monsieur Meyer, urgently called to the scene, comes rushing in. Whatever possessed you to get up on a stepladder at your age? He had the callousness to say publicly: *at your age*. Then he turns to the new secretary and murmurs something I can't quite make out, but his hostility doesn't escape me. Not a word of consolation from him.

Today, peace has begun to return to my life as it once again assumes its normal order. The temporary seclusion that my fracture caused me has kept me safe and out of harm's way. Far from the Agency. Far from Monsieur

Meyer. Far from the new secretary and her quarrelsome ways, which, I can say without exaggeration, are the cause of my present state of affairs.

This isolation has afforded me such a sense of freedom, an emotion so close to euphoria that although I've been reduced to getting around in a wheelchair these first few days, instead of feeling depressed or demeaned, I'm having a wonderful time. And when the nurse assigned to wheel me to my X-ray races my chair at top speed, rather than get angry, I burst into a fit of laughter.

There's no denying that the nurses here are hard up for entertainment. One of their favorite little games consists of scaring their wheelchair patients half to death by propelling them around the hospital grounds at breakneck speed, coming to an abrupt halt only a few feet from a barrier. I've heard that some of them have become masters at this odd little sport. Even accomplished some rather elaborate slaloms, it seems.

After those first delightful days, however, the weeks that follow plunge me into a torpor. Incapacitated and bedridden (my only activity consists of smoking, and I smoke incessantly), I'm driven to thoughts that my immobility only serves to make worse, endless, obsessive thoughts that take the shape, face, and voice of the new secretary. Hence, I have the feeling that my extricating myself from the grip of the new secretary, by dint of time and distance, is in fact an illusion, and that she controls me from within, controls my nerves and my blood and keeps me prisoner inside myself. To struggle against her further would amount to waging war against my own life.

My cleaning lady, to whom I carefully explain this bizarre and awful imprisonment, looks at me with a bewilderment that is more depressing than her not believing me. I conclude that she thinks I'm lost, because she's hopelessly inept at following the chain of events that have led me to this impasse, logically, step by step.

I realize a little more each day, in fact, the impossibility of making others understand the cross the new secretary has given me to bear with utter impunity. A commonplace ordeal, all in all. No clanking of chains, no corpses, no bats in the dark. In fact, I might be better off not confiding in anyone at all, carrying on my crusade in solitude, seeking counsel in no one but myself, though I realize that in the long term, the strain on my powers of reason might prove too great, and I risk being driven around the bend by my own obsession.

Now that my cast has been removed, I'm authorized to take part in the numerous activities highlighted in the clinic's three-color brochure.

Not being a swimmer, I'm a bit apprehensive when I go to the pool, and I've never set foot in such unsavory places as public pools.

I take my place in line. All around me, I see nothing but old people. The whole pool has been invaded by old people. I inch ahead. But faced with these golden-agers in ruins, half-mad and impotent, this flaccid, sallow flesh, I can't help but recoil. Cynically cruel thoughts come into my head. All these old bodies floundering about in the different pools, wearing the same hospital-issue yellow plastic bathing caps, which adds a comic note to this hideous *tableau vivant*. I inch forward again, my legs trembling. The physical therapist grabs me by the hand and pushes me into the bubbling water. Everybody hop up and down! he shouts. I feel terribly clumsy, all brittle bones and frayed muscles. Everybody hop up and down! I hop up and down, pathetically. I wish the earth would swallow me up. Have you ever tried to hop up and down in water? Let's hold on to the rail, hold on to the rail! shouts the therapist. I hold on to the rail. I'm terrified at the idea of falling down again. Let's slowly bend our knees now, slowly! In a pool next to mine, a spindly old woman seems riveted to the wall by a powerful water hose that an expressionless young man is aiming at her. Her frail body twitches with little spasmodic jolts until

I'm sure she's going to fall and shatter. Slowly, shouts the therapist. I slowly bend my knees, almost sick at heart. Before me, I see nothing but hunched, unsteady backs, bones showing through the skin. I slowly stand back up, while a silent sob, coming from some depth within me, rises through my breast.

My rehabilitation schedule indicates a calisthenics class for this afternoon. Must I attend? I'm reluctant. This morning's ordeal has broken my morale. For the first time, the idea of irreversible decrepitude looms, and I dread having to face it again. But my sense of discipline wins the day. I decide to follow the doctor's orders to the letter. I expect somehow that this obedience will earn me some sort of reward. But then, I've always enjoyed obeying.

The outfits worn by the participants already busy exercising are widely varied. The more fashionable women wear colorful tracksuits. The brazen blondes are in trousers. Most of the women are dressed like me in a skirt or dress. (I have never worn trousers. I respect my gender.) The gym teacher seems to be paying no attention to his class. He makes a series of unconvincing arm movements that we all immediately imitate. The mood is a cheerful one. The trainer looks at us patients as if we were some curious form of beetle. Far from offending the participants, this attitude makes us laugh. I start to relax little by little. I forget this morning's feeling of looming disaster. I execute a few silly floor exercises, then lay prostrate on the ground, having abandoned all sense of dignity. The trainer shouts: on your feet. A large number of the participants, myself included, are unable to get back up. Our fruitless, random movements set off a storm of giggles among us. The trainer's face remains expressionless, which only makes matters worse, as we roll with a contagious laughter that sweeps away all my woes. The more able-bodied among us help the others, still shaking on the floor like upturned cockroaches, to slowly get to their feet. Put your arms to your sides and one, two, one, two.

I get back to my room, feeling revived and alert. I'm surprised to find I'm now sharing it with an elderly woman whose complexion and hair are the same ashen color. Suddenly, before I have time to react, she grabs my jacket, slips it on over her nightdress and takes off down the hallway.

A few minutes later, two male nurses bring her back, dragging her by the wrists, and caution me to lock up all my personal belongings.

Hardly a quarter of an hour has passed when my roommate sits up, a fierce look on her face, and announces that she's leaving. I'm not sure whose side to take. Should I call the nurses? Try to detain her through persuasion or force? I'm still weighing the matter when she's already gone.

She returns flanked by the two nurses, who shove her brutally by the shoulders. We're getting a little fed up with this, granny, says the shorter of the two, with a Corsican accent.

At precisely 6:00 P.M. an orderly brings us a meal with no salt, no pepper, no sauce, no anything. She sits on my roommate's bed and shovels spoonfuls of some revolting purée into her mouth. At first, the old woman lets herself be force-fed, but she soon refuses. The orderly tries to pry her teeth open with the spoon, but she might as well be trying to force open a cadaver's jaws.

The orderly leaves. My roommate is crying. I'm suddenly so miserable that I can't face having to console her. My daughter phones.

It's not going well at all, I tell her. Another day here will be the death of me. You're exaggerating, as usual, says my daughter. She promises to come see me on Sunday. Five endless days until Sunday. You'll come to see me on Sunday? You swear on your mother's head?

While I'm talking to my daughter, my roommate slips out yet again. This little game has gone on long enough, shouts the Corsican, shoving her back into the room. Without the slightest compunction, the two nurses pin her to the mattress and tie her wrists to the bedposts with Ace bandages.

The knife-like pain in my heart begins again. Untie me, my neighbor begs me; can't you see I'm suffering? I'm wracked with guilt. I'd like to come to her rescue, but I worry about the consequences. In the end, I tell her I don't have the right, and that I've always obeyed rules, less out of fear, mind you, than a sense of discipline. The old hag hurls curses at me, the likes of which I've never heard. Her face is hideously contorted. She looks dead. I start thinking about my own escape. This place will sap what little is left of me if I don't. Why won't my daughter understand? The old woman pursues her foul litany, finally forgets about me and starts in on her children, only to finish by babbling incoherently to herself in a language filled with swear words and obscenities, interrupted by bursts of laughter and silent dismay during which she recovers a bit of her humanity. She babbles on like this for most of the night without ever managing to achieve self-awareness, or even forgiveness.

The next morning, I go sit on a bench somewhere on the grounds, where I end up spending most of the day.

A wreck.

At five, my cleaning lady visits me, but she can stay only a few minutes, because the strictly regimented visiting hours are nearly over. It's worse than during the war, she says, indignantly. At least in the Argelès camp, we went to bed when we pleased. Of course, she snickers, there wasn't much room, not a whole lot of privacy, especially when you needed to take a crap, she adds, with her customary coarseness.

Before leaving, she places on the nightstand, next to the undergarments I asked her to purchase for me, a bar of chocolate with hazelnuts and a packet of Belin butter cookies. I devour them.

On Thursday, the unexpected arrival of Monsieur Longuet provides some solace. After catching up on my latest news, he offers to get us something to drink from the vending machines. He returns with one coffee. This place is horrible, I tell him. The nurses are sadists. I'm going to write a letter to the editor of *Libération*. Monsieur Longuet then taps me on the hand; this otherwise innocuous gesture, in some mysterious way, goes straight to my heart.

21.

Since my coming home from the clinic, Monsieur Longuet and my cleaning lady have been killing me with so much insincere kindness, showing me so much fake thoughtfulness, that at times I feel like I must be carrying some undetected but fatal disease that makes me worthy of all their consideration and attention. They'll coddle me to an early grave.

They're right, in a way. Mine is an incurable illness. And each time I think about going back to work, I'm filled with dread. I know that she'll be waiting for me— that the end is inexorably drawing near.

Today, the doctor stopped by around three. My cleaning lady and Monsieur Longuet took up positions on either side of my armchair, wearing forced expressions of consternation. Unless you do some regular physical therapy, the doctor warned, your ankle is going to go numb and osteoarthritis will inevitably set in. Osteoarthritis! cried my cleaning lady, looking terrified. In the boundless inventory of human misery that she tirelessly delights in exploring, osteoarthritis holds a privileged position (second place after giving birth). Whenever I put my hands in cold water, it's like having my fingernails pulled out, she moans, deliberately trying to make me feel guilty, and my back is even worse. The pain starts here (she points to the nape of her neck) and goes all the way to here (tracing a half circle in the air that ends at her tailbone).

Once the doctor has left, Monsieur Longuet, speaking in his official capacity, lets me know that, due to the roadwork outside the building, the water will be cut off next Monday. I've been keeping an eye on those workers from my window, and I can tell you that they've been at those pipelines for three months, three months I tell you, and they're not making any progress, not an inch. He catches his breath. There's an Arab down there who uses his shovel like a teaspoon. My cleaning lady laughs hysterically. Egged on, Monsieur Longuet mimes the Arab worker digging and dumping spoonfuls of dirt, raising his little pinky. At this, my cleaning lady is in stitches, with an abandon that can only be described as sexual.

I despise both of them.

I return to work on Friday, the first of February. It's freezing outside. The city is frozen solid. The rigid tree branches oddly resemble the outstretched arms of death, ready to close. I have trouble walking. Dear Lord, what a miracle that we manage on certain days to place one foot in front of the other. I enter the office and there she is, ruling the roost. Her face feigns neutrality. But I know she's been waiting for me. Glad to see you back, she declares. She asks about my ankle, trying to be amiable, to allay my suspicions. She then offers to teach me how to use a Macintosh. It takes me a few seconds to realize that my typewriter has been removed. I had been the only person left in the office to enjoy the privilege of using a typewriter. I feel myself going weak. My legs no longer support my weight, and I sit down. Now let me show you how this thing works; it's easy as can be—you'll see. She's hoping to win hands down now. I refuse outright, for the first time. She insists. She read in *Femme Actuelle* that most writers nowadays use computers. The mediocre ones, I say.

I'm given little work to do for the first week. I take advantage of the free time to indulge in my much-neglected favorite activity: tidying up. I tidy up my drawers and cabinets as if I were about to leave on a long trip. The new secretary keeps insisting I should pace myself, take it easy, you only live once, and all that. She spares no effort to win me over, get on my good side, lull me into complacency. But I'm quick to understand that this incitement to idleness is only a ruse, all the better to accuse me of carelessness down the road.

Monsieur Meyer comes in and asks the new secretary how far along she's come on the perfume file, the ESCAPE: THE SCENT OF FREEDOM report. Then he turns toward me. So, how was our Suzanne's little vacation? He seems to have forgotten that I was hospitalized for over a month. On his way out, he says, almost as an afterthought, Suzanne dear, when you've got a minute, would you stop by my office? There are a couple things we have to talk about. I repeat that sentence to myself a hundred times throughout the day, examining it from every angle, trying to foresee all the eventual repercussions. My mind floods with a sense of doom. The wildest ideas. I consider resigning on the spot.

My daughter comes for a visit. Since my stay at the clinic, she stops by every Friday from seven to eight in the evening to perform her good deed of the week, to look in on the poor. She's seated, flipping through a copy of *Paris Match*. I'm itching to report Monsieur Meyer's mysterious phrase, which is still at the forefront of my concerns. But I don't dare. Nothing I have to say seems to meet with her approval. So I speak of nothing but the most boring trivialities, further justifying her nasty mood. My daughter puts down her magazine. Soon she'll start showing impatience. She suddenly realizes that she's in a terrible hurry, that all sorts of little chores await her at home. Whenever my daughter comes for a visit, she's in a terrible hurry. Her self-imposed visitation duty fuels a resentment that she is at pains to disguise, but which always erupts at the first excuse. She visits against her will, playing the devoted daughter, but only out of cowardice and force of habit. I sense that my daughter's only attachment to me now is a leash of habit that is strangling her. It's time she were unleashed, I conclude. But how can I reconcile myself to breaking this tie that has always anchored me so firmly to the earth? I'd rather make do with her guilt-ridden, compulsory visits, offered grudgingly, and which I wrongly believe are better than nothing.

I walk my daughter down to the door. In the foyer, Messieurs Longuet and Arnaud are in full debate, arms gesticulating wildly. Monsieur Arnaud is holding a bird-cage in which he's stuffed his poodle. The dog takes up the entire cage, which looks like a kind of girdle, his paws dangling out the sides. Some little creep nearly ran right over him, rages Monsieur Arnaud. On purpose, adds Monsieur Longuet smugly.

I wait to be alone with Monsieur Longuet to announce to him my intention to resign. He rejoices. It's just what those scum deserve! That'll teach them! And he sets about drawing up a schedule of leisure activities for my new life, appointing himself as the chief coordinator. In preparation for this vacation, this pre-vacation, he rectifies with a bronchial laugh, we could go tomorrow to visit a monument. The Louvre, for instance. I've heard they've built a kind of crystal pyramid in the courtyard. Crystal? Crystal! asserts Monsieur Longuet. Saturday my cleaning lady comes. Who'll keep an eye on her? A discussion ensues, and I finally decide to go along with the visit to the Louvre and its pyramid.

Saturday at nine sharp, Monsieur Longuet rings the doorbell. We'll take the metro, he suggests, now that we're both living on a pension . . . if you call this living. At which he bursts into uncontrolled laughter. We walk to the Châtelet station. The platform is packed. Monsieur Longuet tells me to move away from the edge because he read that weirdoes that you run into everywhere in big cities have been known to push people onto the rails where they are crushed to death in unspeakable agony. Why did I ever accept his invitation? I'm regretting it already. Once on the train, I'm sandwiched between a fat man on one side and a skinny young one on the other. The swaying of the train forces me to lean at times against the belly of the fat one, whose every breath shakes his stomach, and at other times against the thin one, just like the most squalid of pornographic films. A shady-looking young woman sings an a capella rendition of a Patricia Kaas song, in an ugly, off-key voice, greeted by utter indifference. At the end of the song, she passes through the compartment and stops in front of each passenger, hand extended. Most of them pretend not to see the woman standing right in front of them. Monsieur Meyer's phrase comes suddenly back to mind.

At the Louvre station, we're thrown out onto the platform by a human wave of overwhelming force. We take the escalator up. Once at the top, I don't know how to get off the escalator, and I stagger. Monsieur Longuet catches me by the elbow. You'd better not make a habit of falling flat on your face.

I'm feeling too weary to visit the museum. We go into a café and order two decafs. Twenty francs, says the waiter. Monsieur Longuet rushes to take the check, but can't help saying that we could have bought a whole packet of the best coffee for the same amount. One hundred percent Arabica.

I get home, exhausted. My daughter phones to let me know that she'll be leaving to spend eight days in Brazil with her husband who's attending an international cardiology convention. I'm not mentally prepared for this news and my reaction is inappropriate and absurd. Be careful not to get sunstroke, I say. It happens before you know it, adds my cleaning lady. My daughter hangs up. I think there's something I forgot to tell her.

Going down the stairs, I overhear a muted conversation between Monsieur Longuet and my cleaning lady, who used the excuse of an errand at the butcher's to go gossip. With the old lady, if you know how to handle her, she'll go along with whatever you want, my cleaning lady says. She's a good sort, if you know how to handle her. One thing I've figured out is that you have to stand up to her, get her riled—it makes her think she's in charge. If she says white, I say black, if she says left, I say right—or the other way around, says my cleaning lady with a laugh. But if the old lady ends up broke, no skin off my nose. And the daughter, now that she knows there's nothing more to get out of her (my cleaning lady counts out invisible money), it's *bella ciao, bambino*. And who's gonna be stuck with her then?

I flee, so as not to hear the rest.

22.

My dear Suzanne, begins Monsieur Meyer in an unctuous tone, it's my policy to inform every employee under my orders, . . . er, under my roof, that is, of their full entitlements. Now, you may be unaware, my dear Suzanne, that for the ailing or burned-out who are closing in on sixty, there are—no, no, don't protest, my dear Suzanne, he hastens to say, I won't have a bit of it; I know what you're going to say, I know you very well—how long has it been? Thirty years? Thirty-two, you say. Time passes so quickly, doesn't it? Anyway, we have a provision for the ailing and the burnouts, and you do fit that category, my dear Suzanne. Don't say that you don't, because I know you do, and I can assure you that it pains me; one gets attached to one's employees, what can I say . . . So, as I was explaining, there's the option for an early retirement that offers nearly all the benefits of a normal retirement. Ah, ah! no objections, please. I won't hear of it. We're all concerned about your health, my dear Suzanne; it's for your own good that we're considering this option, believe me. All I ask is that you think it over carefully, he says, rising from his chair.

It all happened very fast. I went back to my office, my

mind a blank. I entered the office, and there she was, with that look of triumph. I flew at her, grabbing her by the hair. I pulled with all my might. I feared nothing now. She began to scream. I screamed louder than she did. An endless scream. People came rushing and tried to get me to let go. I pushed them away with a newfound strength. More staff arrived. Monsieur Meyer came running. What the hell is going on here? he asked. This is all we needed.

I won't speak of the events that followed. May they remain in the murky depths from which they arose. I'll say only that I was thrown out like a pile of dirty clothes. Dumped. After thirty years, no, thirty-two years of service. Should I regret it? Should I rejoice? I don't know, and I don't care.

My daughter came to see me yesterday, and announced that she's going to have a baby. Maybe this will bring us closer together again, she said. At that, I did something unexpected: I hugged my daughter to my heart, with a burst of pity and tenderness that I had never in my life expressed. And my daughter responded to my embrace. She kissed me lightly on the cheek and looked at me through teary eyes, cleansed of all anger.

It's three in the afternoon. The housework is finished. I still haven't figured out how to fill my days. In the end, television tires my eyes, and I've lost my taste for reading. The hardest moment for me comes in the early evening, between four and seven. It seems each time that I'll never make it through. When my time comes, it will happen between four and seven. Most often, I sit in a chair and do nothing. I'm shrinking; at least that's my impression. My son-in-law the doctor broadcasts to all and sundry that I'm suffering from nervous prostration. Well, I say that it's simply an excess of inactivity brought about by terrible circumstances entirely beyond my control.

Saturday afternoon goes by faster than other days. Monsieur Longuet, my cleaning lady, and myself, we play gin rummy every Saturday. I really enjoy these games of rummy. They allow me to exercise my brain and my tongue, which I sometimes fear will atrophy from sheer disuse. I very much enjoy these card parties, but I find one detail exasperating: I have to watch my partners like a hawk to make sure they don't cheat. Can I trust an illiterate Spanish cleaning lady and a sick, retired widower, who arouses a condescending pity in everyone?

About the Author

Lydie Salvayre, the daughter of refugees from the Spanish Civil War, grew up in the south of France, where she attended medical school and received a degree in psychiatry. She has published twelve other novels, including *The Company of Ghosts*, *The Lecture*, and *The Power of Flies*.

SELECTED DALKEY ARCHIVE PAPERBACKS

Petros Abatzoglou, *What Does Mrs. Freeman Want?*
Pierre Albert-Birot, *Grabinoulor.*
Yuz Aleshkovsky, *Kangaroo.*
Felipe Alfau, *Chromos.*
    Locos.
Ivan Ângelo, *The Celebration.*
    The Tower of Glass.
David Antin, *Talking.*
Djuna Barnes, *Ladies Almanack.*
    Ryder.
John Barth, *LETTERS.*
    Sabbatical.
Donald Barthelme, *The King.*
    Paradise.
Svetislav Basara, *Chinese Letter.*
Mark Binelli, *Sacco and Vanzetti Must Die!*
Andrei Bitov, *Pushkin House.*
Louis Paul Boon, *Chapel Road.*
    Summer in Termuren.
Roger Boylan, *Killoyle.*
Ignácio de Loyola Brandão, *Teeth under the Sun.*
    Zero.
Christine Brooke-Rose, *Amalgamemnon.*
Brigid Brophy, *In Transit.*
Meredith Brosnan, *Mr. Dynamite.*
Gerald L. Bruns,
    Modern Poetry and the Idea of Language.
Gabrielle Burton, *Heartbreak Hotel.*
Michel Butor, *Degrees.*
    Mobile.
    Portrait of the Artist as a Young Ape.
G. Cabrera Infante, *Infante's Inferno.*
    Three Trapped Tigers.
Julieta Campos, *The Fear of Losing Eurydice.*
Anne Carson, *Eros the Bittersweet.*
Camilo José Cela, *The Family of Pascual Duarte.*
    The Hive.
Louis-Ferdinand Céline, *Castle to Castle.*
    Conversations with Professor Y.
    London Bridge.
    North.
    Rigadoon.
Hugo Charteris, *The Tide Is Right.*
Jerome Charyn, *The Tar Baby.*
Marc Cholodenko, *Mordechai Schamz.*
Emily Holmes Coleman, *The Shutter of Snow.*
Robert Coover, *A Night at the Movies.*
Stanley Crawford, *Some Instructions to My Wife.*
Robert Creeley, *Collected Prose.*
René Crevel, *Putting My Foot in It.*
Ralph Cusack, *Cadenza.*
Susan Daitch, *L.C.*
    Storytown.
Nigel Dennis, *Cards of Identity.*
Peter Dimock,
    A Short Rhetoric for Leaving the Family.
Ariel Dorfman, *Konfidenz.*
Coleman Dowell, *The Houses of Children.*
    Island People.
    Too Much Flesh and Jabez.
Rikki Ducornet, *The Complete Butcher's Tales.*
    The Fountains of Neptune.
    The Jade Cabinet.
    Phosphor in Dreamland.
    The Stain.
    The Word "Desire."
William Eastlake, *The Bamboo Bed.*
    Castle Keep.
    Lyric of the Circle Heart.
Jean Echenoz, *Chopin's Move.*
Stanley Elkin, *A Bad Man.*
    Boswell: A Modern Comedy.
    Criers and Kibitzers, Kibitzers and Criers.
    The Dick Gibson Show.
    The Franchiser.
    George Mills.
    The Living End.
    The MacGuffin.
    The Magic Kingdom.
    Mrs. Ted Bliss.
    The Rabbi of Lud.
    Van Gogh's Room at Arles.
Annie Ernaux, *Cleaned Out.*
Lauren Fairbanks, *Muzzle Thyself.*
    Sister Carrie.
Leslie A. Fiedler,
    Love and Death in the American Novel.
Gustave Flaubert, *Bouvard and Pécuchet.*
Ford Madox Ford, *The March of Literature.*
Jon Fosse, *Melancholy.*
Max Frisch, *I'm Not Stiller.*
Carlos Fuentes, *Christopher Unborn.*
    Distant Relations.
    Terra Nostra.
    Where the Air Is Clear.
Janice Galloway, *Foreign Parts.*
    The Trick Is to Keep Breathing.
William H. Gass, *The Tunnel.*
    Willie Masters' Lonesome Wife.
Etienne Gilson, *The Arts of the Beautiful.*
    Forms and Substances in the Arts.
C. S. Giscombe, *Giscome Road.*
    Here.
Douglas Glover, *Bad News of the Heart.*
    The Enamoured Knight.
Karen Elizabeth Gordon, *The Red Shoes.*
Georgi Gospodinov, *Natural Novel.*
Juan Goytisolo, *Marks of Identity.*
Patrick Grainville, *The Cave of Heaven.*
Henry Green, *Blindness.*
    Concluding.
    Doting.
    Nothing.
Jiří Gruša, *The Questionnaire.*
John Hawkes, *Whistlejacket.*
Aidan Higgins, *A Bestiary.*
    Bornholm Night-Ferry.
    Flotsam and Jetsam.
    Langrishe, Go Down.
    Scenes from a Receding Past.
    Windy Arbours.
Aldous Huxley, *Antic Hay.*
    Crome Yellow.
    Point Counter Point.
    Those Barren Leaves.
    Time Must Have a Stop.
Mikhail Iossel and Jeff Parker, eds., *Amerika:*
    Contemporary Russians View
    the United States.
Gert Jonke, *Geometric Regional Novel.*
Jacques Jouet, *Mountain R.*
Hugh Kenner, *The Counterfeiters.*
    Flaubert, Joyce and Beckett:
    The Stoic Comedians.
    Joyce's Voices.
Danilo Kiš, *Garden, Ashes.*
    A Tomb for Boris Davidovich.
Anita Konkka, *A Fool's Paradise.*
Tadeusz Konwicki, *A Minor Apocalypse.*
    The Polish Complex.
Menis Koumandareas, *Koula.*
Elaine Kraf, *The Princess of 72nd Street.*
Jim Krusoe, *Iceland.*
Ewa Kuryluk, *Century 21.*
Violette Leduc, *La Bâtarde.*
Deborah Levy, *Billy and Girl.*
    Pillow Talk in Europe and Other Places.
José Lezama Lima, *Paradiso.*
Rosa Liksom, *Dark Paradise.*
Osman Lins, *Avalovara.*
    The Queen of the Prisons of Greece.
Alf Mac Lochlainn, *The Corpus in the Library.*
    Out of Focus.
Ron Loewinsohn, *Magnetic Field(s).*
D. Keith Mano, *Take Five.*
Ben Marcus, *The Age of Wire and String.*
Wallace Markfield, *Teitlebaum's Window.*
    To an Early Grave.
David Markson, *Reader's Block.*
    Springer's Progress.
    Wittgenstein's Mistress.

SELECTED DALKEY ARCHIVE PAPERBACKS

CAROLE MASO, *AVA.*

LADISLAV MATEJKA AND KRYSTYNA POMORSKA, EDS., *Readings in Russian Poetics: Formalist and Structuralist Views.*

HARRY MATHEWS,
The Case of the Persevering Maltese: Collected Essays.
Cigarettes.
The Conversions.
The Human Country: New and Collected Stories.
The Journalist.
My Life in CIA.
Singular Pleasures.
The Sinking of the Odradek Stadium.
Tlooth.
20 Lines a Day.

ROBERT L. MCLAUGHLIN, ED.,
Innovations: An Anthology of Modern & Contemporary Fiction.

HERMAN MELVILLE, *The Confidence-Man.*

STEVEN MILLHAUSER, *The Barnum Museum.*
In the Penny Arcade.

RALPH J. MILLS, JR., *Essays on Poetry.*

OLIVE MOORE, *Spleen.*

NICHOLAS MOSLEY, *Accident.*
Assassins.
Catastrophe Practice.
Children of Darkness and Light.
Experience and Religion.
The Hesperides Tree.
Hopeful Monsters.
Imago Bird.
Impossible Object.
Inventing God.
Judith.
Look at the Dark.
Natalie Natalia.
Serpent.
Time at War.
The Uses of Slime Mould: Essays of Four Decades.

WARREN F. MOTTE, JR.,
Fables of the Novel: French Fiction since 1990.
Oulipo: A Primer of Potential Literature.

YVES NAVARRE, *Our Share of Time.*
Sweet Tooth.

DOROTHY NELSON, *In Night's City.*
Tar and Feathers.

WILFRIDO D. NOLLEDO, *But for the Lovers.*

FLANN O'BRIEN, *At Swim-Two-Birds.*
At War.
The Best of Myles.
The Dalkey Archive.
Further Cuttings.
The Hard Life.
The Poor Mouth.
The Third Policeman.

CLAUDE OLLIER, *The Mise-en-Scène.*

PATRIK OUŘEDNÍK, *Europeana.*

FERNANDO DEL PASO, *Palinuro of Mexico.*

ROBERT PINGET, *The Inquisitory.*
Mahu or The Material.
Trio.

RAYMOND QUENEAU, *The Last Days.*
Odile.
Pierrot Mon Ami.
Saint Glinglin.

ANN QUIN, *Berg.*
Passages.
Three.
Tripticks.

ISHMAEL REED, *The Free-Lance Pallbearers.*
The Last Days of Louisiana Red.
Reckless Eyeballing.
The Terrible Threes.
The Terrible Twos.
Yellow Back Radio Broke-Down.

JULIÁN RÍOS, *Larva: A Midsummer Night's Babel.*
Poundemonium.

AUGUSTO ROA BASTOS, *I the Supreme.*

JACQUES ROUBAUD, *The Great Fire of London.*
Hortense in Exile.

Hortense Is Abducted.
The Plurality of Worlds of Lewis.
The Princess Hoppy.
The Form of a City Changes Faster, Alas, Than the Human Heart.
Some Thing Black.

LEON S. ROUDIEZ, *French Fiction Revisited.*

VEDRANA RUDAN, *Night.*

LYDIE SALVAYRE, *The Company of Ghosts.*
Everyday Life.
The Lecture.

LUIS RAFAEL SÁNCHEZ, *Macho Camacho's Beat.*

SEVERO SARDUY, *Cobra & Maitreya.*

NATHALIE SARRAUTE, *Do You Hear Them?*
Martereau.
The Planetarium.

ARNO SCHMIDT, *Collected Stories.*
Nobodaddy's Children.

CHRISTINE SCHUTT, *Nightwork.*

GAIL SCOTT, *My Paris.*

JUNE AKERS SEESE,
Is This What Other Women Feel Too?
What Waiting Really Means.

AURELIE SHEEHAN, *Jack Kerouac Is Pregnant.*

VIKTOR SHKLOVSKY, *Knight's Move.*
A Sentimental Journey: Memoirs 1917-1922.
Theory of Prose.
Third Factory.
Zoo, or Letters Not about Love.

JOSEF ŠKVORECKÝ,
The Engineer of Human Souls.

CLAUDE SIMON, *The Invitation.*

GILBERT SORRENTINO, *Aberration of Starlight.*
Blue Pastoral.
Crystal Vision.
Imaginative Qualities of Actual Things.
Mulligan Stew.
Pack of Lies.
Red the Fiend.
The Sky Changes.
Something Said.
Splendide-Hôtel.
Steelwork.
Under the Shadow.

W. M. SPACKMAN, *The Complete Fiction.*

GERTRUDE STEIN, *Lucy Church Amiably.*
The Making of Americans.
A Novel of Thank You.

PIOTR SZEWC, *Annihilation.*

STEFAN THEMERSON, *Hobson's Island.*
The Mystery of the Sardine.
Tom Harris.

JEAN-PHILIPPE TOUSSAINT, *Television.*

DUMITRU TSEPENEAG, *Vain Art of the Fugue.*

ESTHER TUSQUETS, *Stranded.*

DUBRAVKA UGRESIC, *Lend Me Your Character.*
Thank You for Not Reading.

MATI UNT, *Things in the Night.*

ELOY URROZ, *The Obstacles.*

LUISA VALENZUELA, *He Who Searches.*

BORIS VIAN, *Heartsnatcher.*

PAUL WEST, *Words for a Deaf Daughter & Gala.*

CURTIS WHITE, *America's Magic Mountain.*
The Idea of Home.
Memories of My Father Watching TV.
Monstrous Possibility: An Invitation to Literary Politics.
Requiem.

DIANE WILLIAMS, *Excitability: Selected Stories.*
Romancer Erector.

DOUGLAS WOOLF, *Wall to Wall.*
Ya! & John-Juan.

PHILIP WYLIE, *Generation of Vipers.*

MARGUERITE YOUNG, *Angel in the Forest.*
Miss MacIntosh, My Darling.

REYOUNG, *Unbabbling.*

ZORAN ŽIVKOVIĆ, *Hidden Camera.*

LOUIS ZUKOFSKY, *Collected Fiction.*

SCOTT ZWIREN, *God Head.*

FOR A FULL LIST OF PUBLICATIONS, VISIT:
www.dalkeyarchive.com